RAZE HELL

VIPEROUS

ANATHEMA — BOOK THREE

Yolanda Olson

Jennifer Bene

ISBN (e-book): 978-1-946722-72-0

ISBN (paperback): 978-1-946722-73-7

Cover design by Dez Purington, http://prettyininkcreations.com/

 Created with Vellum

Anathema Series

Noxious

Mephitic

Viperous

ONE

A Promise Broken

LAKYN

I've been staring out the windshield for the past thirty minutes in a daze. I got back to Mesa about an hour ago, but I'm parked a street over from my house turning everything over and over in my head for the hundredth time.

The shit that I just went through fucked with me more than it should have, and I don't know how I'm supposed to walk into my home like everything is okay.

I begin to pick at my fingernails as I think of the upside of things. Red and the kid are gone, which means my life might actually start to return to my spectacular version of normal. The downside of things is that Trixie doesn't remember me or Ichabod, and that's not going to be easy to explain. Fucking impossible, actually, because Ich has had a hard-on for Trixie since before I even met him, and even though my dick is all he wants now I know he'll lose it over this shit.

Leaning my head back against the headrest, I blow out my breath. I know I can't fucking stay here forever, especially not since the asshole that apparently lives here is honking for me to get out of his spot, but it would be nice to be able to steer clear of the old ball and chain until I could figure things out.

"Yeah, yeah," I grumble as I sit up and turn the key. Running a hand back through my hair, I glance in the mirror before I pull away and head over to my place.

"JESUS CHRIST," I mutter as I pull the truck into the driveway. It seems that Ichabod has been staking out the window because it's almost midnight but as soon as I pull in, the curtains shift, and I see his face briefly.

Clearing my throat, I retrieve the keys and tuck them into my pocket before I push the truck door open and step out.

I'm not in the mood for this, I think as soon as the front door swings open and he steps out onto the porch.

A brief glance in his direction and I immediately want to get back into the truck and leave again.

His hair is neatly combed.

He's wearing black slacks and a long-sleeved black shirt, and his newest dress shoes.

If I didn't know any better, I'd say he's wearing his Sunday best, but that's not what's bothering me.

It's the fucking look I catch in his eye. The one of hope that the one person that he was always so desperate to have love him has finally come home to roost.

And now I have to tell him that she's sitting on a completely different nest in Fuck-knows-where Middle of the Desert.

"Hey," I say to him when I get my feet to start shifting. I do my best to keep my stride as confident as it always is and flash him the best smile that I can.

"Hey," he calls back, waving at me. But his eyes are locked on the truck still and I know that his little Goodyear blimp of hope is about to go down like the fucking Hindenburg.

He cranes his neck and I sidestep to stay in his line of sight. His shoulders go limp almost instantly, his eyes darken, and I can see his lips morph into a tight line.

Oh yeah, this is gonna be fun.

"Where's Bea?" he asks in a loud voice that I would almost mistake for a shout if he had the balls for that kind of shit.

"Go inside. I don't want the neighbors gawking at us because you got your period while I was gone," I snap at him as I breeze by and grab him by the elbow to haul him inside.

Ichabod digs his heels into the porch, but one hard yank and the skinny little fucker damn near tumbles into the house. He trips and stumbles but manages to stay on his feet and slam the door shut in response to me coming home emptyhanded.

Fucking fantastic.

I walk into the living room completely determined not to lose my shit on him and sink down into my favorite chair.

Reaching for the pack of smokes I left by the ashtray, I shake one out. Before I have the chance to light it, Ichabod comes over and slaps it out my mouth.

I grind my teeth, square my jaw, and get to my feet. Ichabod doesn't take the step back that I expect him to, instead, he balls his fists at his sides and mimics my anger.

It's almost like looking into a mirror.

Huh. Isn't that what the kid said?

I crack my neck and walk over to where the cigarette ricocheted off the couch and go back to my chair.

When I try to light it, I realize it's broken, and I sigh.

"Where's Bea?" he asks again in a slightly more acceptable tone.

"I couldn't find her."

"You're a liar!" he shouts, trembling with rage instead of the vague sheen of anxiety he normally wears when he gets feisty.

I arch an eyebrow as I look up at him. Of all the time he's spent with me, he should know *that* is the one thing I'll never be.

"What makes you think that?" I ask him tiredly as I shake another smoke out and clench it between my teeth.

When I see Ichabod take a step toward me, I throw a small pillow at him to keep him from breaking this one too.

"Because Aftyn and Daphne aren't here," he barks. I roll my eyes. In what world that makes sense to anyone other than him is beyond me, but ever since he got off the smack, he's been a lot more aware of his surroundings.

I blow out my breath before I take a drag off my smoke and roll my eyes. "Maybe they got smart and decided to fuck off after I got lost."

"Or maybe you're lying!" he screeches at me.

I sit up a little in my chair, smooth out my jeans and tilt my head toward to the left.

"What do you want me to say right now?" I ask him, my patience starting to wear thin.

He comes over and angrily kicks the chair between my legs, probably expecting me to react, and when I don't, he picks up my ashtray and lobs it through the window behind me, shattering it with a loud crash.

"You don't have a job I don't know about, do you?" I ask without turning around to survey the damage.

"What?" he asks in frustration.

"Well, you just busted my window. Someone is gonna have to pay for that," I reply with a shrug.

"How about the same price I always fucking pay?"

I'm confused until he begins to undo his belt, whips it across the room, and drops his pants. Normally, I'd take him up on this offer, but I'm not feeling very frisky at the moment.

Not even when he turns around and yanks his skivvies down to his ankles.

"Do us both a favor and put your clothes back on," I say as I look away. Frisky or not, I'm not exactly one to turn down the offer of a free hole, but I'd hurt him way more than he's used to right now and that would put him out of commission for a while.

What fun would it be if I had to take care of myself for a while?

"Admit that you saw her!" he shouts after he pulls his pants back up.

I roll my eyes, take a drag off my smoke, and look him directly in the eyes. "I saw her."

"See? I knew you were lying!"

I clear my throat, take another deep pull, and blow out a stream of smoke.

"What did she say? Did she say something about me? Why isn't she here, Lakyn? You promised!"

I get to my feet, tired of the barrage of bullshit he's throwing at me and take a step toward him.

"You can't hurt me anymore, Lakyn. You wanted my balls to drop? Well, guess what? They're hanging low now, so unless you plan on telling me what Bea said, I suggest you back up."

His tone is low, even, strong.

All the things I never expected from him but kind of always wanted.

And I have the power to ruin his life right now. To tell him that his beloved Bea doesn't give a fuck about him—just like I always said—because she doesn't even remember him.

"Feeling tough?" I ask, blowing a stream of smoke into face.

"You broke your promise, Lakyn!" Ichabod grunts as he uses his strength and shoves me back roughly into my chair. I wish this were a different circumstance because I would be turned on as fuck right now by this little display.

With a chuckle, I shake my head and get back to my feet, giving his arm a slap as I walk by him.

"You're right. Sorry I let you down," I say over my shoulder as I make my way to my room. I expect him to call after me, or continue his tirade about Trixie, but I'm pretty sure I've stunned him into silence when I make it all the way down the hall without a peep.

Once inside, I stub the cigarette out in the ashtray on the dresser, then close the door behind me, flipping the switch in place to lock it and keep him out, or me away from him. It doesn't really matter either way. Turning away from the door I drop onto the bed and toss my arm over my eyes.

Just leave me the fuck alone.

TWO

The Countdown Starts

ICHABOD

I'm shaking as Lakyn walks past me and down the hall, and I can't make myself turn to look until I hear the door shut. I'd been prepared for a hundred different reactions after I slapped the cigarette out of his mouth. I figured he'd laugh, or yell at me, or hit me, or fuck me.

Hell, I'd been prepared to die just to get all of the betrayal off my fucking chest. But that's my own fault. It was stupid of me to believe he'd bring Bea back.

After all these years I should know that hope only serves to eat me alive from the inside out... but I'd let myself feel it anyway.

I'd believed him.

So fucking stupid.

The anger had surprised me, though. I barely remember deciding to slap the cigarette away… it just *happened*. Like once I'd uncorked all of that rage, all of that miserable fucking hope that Bea would be sitting in that SUV when Lakyn finally came home—I hadn't been able to stop.

I'm going to pay for it.

All of it.

I know it, but even though I'm still shaking from the lingering adrenaline and the raw fear that'll hit me as soon as I process what the fuck I've done… I just don't care.

I can't.

Lakyn always says he keeps his promises, but this time he lied. He deserved to know that, even if all I have waiting for me now is more pain. My breath shudders as I force myself to walk down the hall, pausing at the bedroom door to listen.

I don't know what I expected to hear. Maybe him breaking shit, or blaring Blondie, or *something*, but the silence is almost more eerie than just how fucking calm he was when I lost it.

This is bad.

When Lakyn is quiet it's always just the calm before the storm. It's when he's thinking, planning, plotting, and I know it's my death this time. I should welcome it. After all, what the fuck do I have to live for? Another twenty years of being Lakyn Meyer's favorite fuck toy? His clean-up bitch?

No one would sign up for this life.

So why do I still want to live?

The trembling in my hands is way more fear than anger now, and I hate myself for wanting to survive a little longer. I hate myself for thinking that maybe, just maybe, I'll get to see Bea again. Hope is like a fucking cancer, and I'm terminal with it, which only leaves me one choice.

Rapping my knuckles gently on the door, I clear my throat and call out quietly. "Lakyn?"

Only silence answers me so I lick my dry lips and try again.

"Can I come in?"

I wait, straining to hear over the vague hum of the air conditioning, but there's nothing. I grab the doorknob and try to turn it, but it stops almost instantly. Locked.

He locked me out?

This is new. This is definitely new. And about as weird as the fact that Lakyn didn't knock me to the fucking floor when I came at him. He hates it when anyone touches him, and I shoved him into his goddamn chair—but he didn't do anything.

Fuck, he told me *I* was right, which means something is seriously wrong.

Knocking lightly on the door again, I speak a little louder. "Lakyn… are you okay? Listen, I'm sorry I got so upset. I promise I'll tape up the window, just talk to me."

Silence.

The damn house is as silent as when he left me here, alone, promising to bring Bea back with him. Except now he's back, but there's still so much distance between us and somehow that's even worse. I hate it. I hate *him*.

"Lakyn!" I shout, banging my fist against the door, knowing that I'm poking the proverbial bear and fully expecting him to rip the door open and hurt me—but he doesn't. He doesn't even fucking answer me. "Fine! You want to lock yourself in there, do it. I'm leaving."

I take a few steps down the hall before the fear slides down my spine again and I hesitate, looking back at the door. I can almost picture Lakyn busting out of it with that challenging smirk on his face, ready to make me pay for everything I've done. A part of me wants it to happen, because at least then it would be over. It's the waiting that always drives me insane.

When there's nothing except more silence, I follow through on the threat, walking out front and slamming the door behind me so that I'm sure he heard it. Every door in the fucking house shakes when the front door slams—I've felt it enough from the inside—but Lakyn doesn't come outside. There's no movement of the blinds or a flick of the curtains to tell me that he cared enough to look… and I feel lost.

The decision to start walking is about as conscious as slapping the cigarette out of his mouth. I'm on auto-pilot. Or maybe this is a self-destruct sequence counting down and I'm just waiting for the timer to get to zero, so I'll finally be done.

It's the middle of the night, but I've never been afraid of being on the streets. It's the only thing I knew before Bea started helping me out, and the streets of suburban Mesa, Arizona aren't exactly dangerous even after midnight. No, the danger is back inside the house, and I know it will be waiting for me when I return. Whenever Lakyn snaps out of whatever strange mood he's in. I almost lost my life for Beatrix tonight, and I still might, but that's okay because I know she'd give her life for me if it came down to it.

Seeing her again is the only thing that's kept me going all these years, and as long as there's still a chance I don't really have a choice except to keep breathing.

At least until Lakyn decides he's done with me.

Those thoughts keep spinning around in my head, bouncing back and forth as I meander down random sidewalks, losing myself under the night sky. These two ideas are really all I have left in life. The hope that I still have a chance of seeing Bea, and the absolute certainty that one of these days Lakyn will decide I'm not useful enough to keep around anymore.

Honestly, I've been waiting for that for a while now, but I keep going to sleep beside him and waking up next to him. I keep breathing, keep living, keep surviving, because for some reason he wants me to.

I could just leave.

The empty streets and open sky are like an invitation. As if the universe is giving me the chance to get away from Lakyn Meyer, to escape, but as quickly as the thought enters my mind, it leaves just as fast. It's a stupid idea. I know there's nowhere for me to go. I don't have any money, any skills, any life experience beyond the worst shit the world has to offer.

And Lakyn would find me anyway.

He's always been able to track down the people he wanted to, and he's a lot smarter than people give him credit for when they see that charming smile and those killer looks. I fell for it too when I first saw him— and that's how I know there's no hope for me. I could run, but it would be pointless, and the only person I'd want to see is Bea and there's no way in hell Lakyn will tell me where she is.

There's nowhere I even want to go.

I don't have a future that doesn't involve Lakyn Meyer, and I shouldn't expect anything different. I need to stop hoping. I need to stop trying to believe in the possibility of anything good.

The sooner I can let go of all of that, the more tolerable everything will be.

I'M NOT sure how long I've walked, but I'm sure it's been hours, and when I can finally see the house again I'm fully expecting Lakyn to throw the front door open and lean against the frame with that grin on his face that tells me everything I need to know about how bad it's going to hurt once I'm inside.

But I get all the way onto the driveway and there's not a hint of movement from inside. Not a peep from the house. All I've got is the chorus of cicadas and the distant sound of cars.

I don't know if this is a good sign, or a really fucking bad one, but I figure that the least I can do to get back in his good graces—or Lakyn Meyer's version anyway—is to unload the car. I'm not surprised when the back is unlocked, but the huge pile of fabric leaves me confused for a second. It's a cheap pattern, nothing that Lakyn would ever want in his house, but when I pull it back and see the stain of blood on the white sheet underneath I know that he went shopping for something other than new bedding.

"Don't look," I whisper under my breath, but I can't resist peeling the sheet back enough to see the long black hair and the hint of too-pale skin before I catch sight of her face. She's young, pretty, and I wonder if *this* is what kept him busy. If this girl is why he didn't bring Bea back to me. Did he want to keep her? Did he accidentally kill her out of habit? Was his reaction earlier just disappointment at only having me left?

Is that why he didn't fuck me?

I feel sick to my stomach as I bundle her back up and shimmy my arms under the wad of bedding until I manage to lift her. It takes some juggling to get the front door open, but it's the middle of the night and I'm not worried. If anyone were to try and break in here, it would be their funeral.

Well, not a funeral. No one who enters Lakyn's house actually gets a funeral.

They get dissolved in a tub just like Willa did, just like this girl will be. I carry the latest of Lakyn's conquests into his workshop and drop her to the floor to finish unwrapping the mess. Burning the sheets will be easier than anything else, but my stomach clenches when I finally get a look at what he did.

She's cut open from breasts to cunt, and there's a bunch of other stab wounds around the gaping wound. The bloody mess between her legs looks more like one hole instead of two now, and I kick her legs back together just so I don't have to see it.

It only takes me a few minutes to get her situated, pouring the bottles over her in the way Lakyn taught me, and I make a mental note to remind him that we need more— whenever he starts talking to me again anyway.

With the dark-haired girl disappearing off the face of the earth, I head back out to the SUV and grab one of the bags from the back, barely catching the plastic container that almost tumbles onto the pavement. In the dim light of the driveway I can't tell what it is, but I crack the lid on it as I get back to the porch and it takes a minute for my brain to process what the fuck I'm looking at.

It's a heart. A human heart sitting in a plastic container like the leftovers from some fucked-up meal. *God dammit.*

I drop the duffel bag in the living room and head back to the workshop to add the heart to the mess in the tub. It's probably the girl's heart anyway, and Lakyn might be pissed that

I destroyed his keepsake—if that's what it is—but *someone* has to clean up after his shit.

A few more trips and I've got the rest of the bags inside, and I'm pretty sure that several of them belonged to Aftyn and Willa. As I'm putting Lakyn's favorite hatchet back where it belongs, right next to Bea's hatchet, I sink into the chair in the corner and stare at it.

Did he kill Aftyn? Is the kid out there somewhere in a dumpster, or on the side of the road, chopped into pieces because I reached out to him and lured him into his father's web? Just more questions that I want to ask Lakyn, more answers I probably won't get, but I feel the weight of the guilt anyway.

There aren't really a lot of reasons why Lakyn would have the kid's bags unless Aftyn didn't need them anymore, and that's just one more thing that's my fault.

Everyone that meets Lakyn Meyer eventually dies for the privilege, and I'm just waiting for my turn.

Who knows? By morning, maybe my time will finally be up.

THREE

A New Path

AFTYN

I smile at Raindrop as she walks by The Daughter's home. She's wearing a dress similar to one that is worn by their goddess of the desert, though not exactly.

I've noticed that almost everyone here, male and female, try to emulate her in some way. I seem to be the only one that wanted to stay as I was, but that didn't last very long.

It's been two weeks since I finally found the place where I belong, and I couldn't be happier.

Especially now that Lakyn has gone back to fuck knows where—though no one cares about that except for Daphne, and probably his boyfriend. I still think about Ichabod

25

sometimes when I hear the stories of how so many of the Children of the Light escaped bad situations to find this oasis, and I can't help but think about how he would have been happier out here in the desert regardless of Beatrix not remembering him. I would like to think that in due time, all memories—painful or otherwise—serve a purpose and she'd use her newfound happiness to lift him up instead of knocking him down like Pops does.

Of course, he could get away from that fucked-up situation any time he wants to, and he chooses to stay, so I tell myself that it's not my fault.

None of this is.

Not Dexter.

Not Daphne.

Not Lakyn.

I think what's helped me get through the recent trauma I've experienced the most is The Daughter. She looks so much like my Willa, cares about me just as deeply, and holds me so closely any time I cry over her. She's always patient as she helps me to understand that the universe is all-knowing and works in the way it wants… even if it's not in the way one would hope.

It's a concept I'm still struggling with even though so much of it is comforting.

She's explained over our time together that Willa has gone to be a Light Weaver before us and that, eventually, we'll be together again. But for now, I belong to her, on this plane of existence, and I'm okay with that.

While I'm still trying to understand all of her teachings, the one thing I've been able to glean from that shitstorm is that… I did it. With everything that went wrong, in the end I got the one thing Lakyn Meyer always wanted and could never get. And since he took Willa from me, I think it's only fair that I get to keep The Daughter.

It may be her title here, but it still kind of bugs me to call her that, she just doesn't respond to Beatrix, Trixie, or any form of the name. It's just how things are here. She's not that person anymore. She's ascended to a plane where she doesn't need a name, only a title, and to be surrounded by those she's gathered around her to accept her teachings and weave light for the universe.

Even when the water from the Cactus of Ambrosia wears off, she refuses to respond to her given name. She's told me that it's because it's a mortal name and she's no longer of this coil—whatever that means—but I've given up on pressing the issue. She's mine, Lakyn is gone, and that's all that matters.

I tilt my face toward the sky and let out a gentle sigh as the warmth washes over me. It has nothing on her touch, but I can't compare the two. Now that I know Willa is in the light, I understand that she's the warmth I feel on my skin.

That's the comfort that has kept me from leaving. On the very first night that I cried about it, The Daughter explained it all to me. She promised me that it's Willa's light that shines down on me during the day and in the reflection of the moon on the windows at night.

The prickle I feel on my arms when the hair stands up is a gift. It's her sign to let me know that she's with me and always will be.

I glance down at my wrist, looking at the hair tie that means the world to me, and I know that if I ever lose the feeling and knowledge bestowed upon me by The Daughter, I'll still always have a piece of Willa that no one will be able to take away. A permanent connection to my best friend.

But I take solace in knowing the truth that The Daughter has shown to me in ways that I'll never be able to fully appreciate.

The truth that Willa is everywhere, in everything, and *that* is the only truth I'll ever need to believe.

———

"I'M STILL in awe of how long it's been, Lakyn," The Daughter says to me as I sit at the head of her table. Sun Wolf sets a plate of breakfast in front of me while Luminescence does the same with her.

They smile at us, ask us if there's anything else we'll need, and she waves them away, returning the joy plastered on their faces. When I first saw those smiles, I thought they were fake, or that the people here were fools, but now I know better. When I look at The Daughter, I want to smile too. There's something about her that just makes people happier. And it's true for me too… except when she calls me by *his* name.

I let out a sigh and rub the back of my neck uneasily. For the two weeks that I've been here, I've done my best to convince her that I'm *not* Lakyn, but it seems lost on her. The words never quite penetrate, or they're just unimportant to her when compared to everything else she thinks about as The Daughter of the Light—but for once I'd like to hear her use my actual name.

"Tell me, how did you find me?" she asks. "You mentioned something about a woman back home?"

I wait patiently as she raises a flat piece of boiled cactus to her mouth and takes a dainty bite. I haven't gotten used to eating this yet, and I'm not sure if I ever will, but until they have their semi-annual roadside bead sale, it's apparently all we've got. Except for the beans. That's something they can grow easily in the greenhouse, but when I bite into one, it's hard.

I don't want to insult her, or her followers that cooked the meal, so I just grind my teeth down and hope it breaks soon enough.

"Daughter," I begin as I try desperately to swallow down the rock I'm working on grinding down. "I'm not Lakyn. I'm Aftyn, his son."

"I remember your sense of humor," she says with a twinkle in her eye. "I love that you never lost that part about you that shines so brightly."

Right. I blow out my breath as I reach for my knife and fork, severing a piece of the cactus as best as I can. I don't want to insult her. Not after what we've shared here so far. She's been amazing to me and has loved me in ways that no one ever has before—body and soul— which is just one more reason why I really want to hear my name on her perfect lips.

"You've never met me before," I insist, keeping my voice soft and calm. "I wouldn't lie to you... I-I love you."

The Daughter's smile widens. "And I love you as I love all of my children."

I raise an eyebrow.

I would have thought that after spending almost every night in her bed, I would have meant more to her than the rest of her 'children,' but I guess I'll just have to try harder.

"Daughter, please listen to me. I swear to you that I'm not Lakyn Meyer. My name is Aftyn Meyer, my best friend is Willa Banks, and her other best friend was Dexter Holland. We got into a car from New York to drive to Arizona because I… well, I was goaded by someone to go meet Lakyn. It was his, um… boyfriend, I think, but he won't admit it. His name is Ichabod."

As she takes in what I've said to her, she leans back in her chair, eyes closed, hands resting delicately on the wooden arms. At this point, I don't think she even fucking heard me.

"Ichabod… Mr. Meyer said that name to me, but I don't recall ever having met someone by that title. Is he a Weaver of Light that needs to find his way to us?"

I don't want to get frustrated with her, however, I can feel my nerves starting to fray.

Taking a deep breath, I decide it's best to finish breakfast in silence, and we almost do until a few moments later, she gasps so loudly that it startles me and several others nearby.

"Are you okay?" I ask, glancing over at her.

"You're... you're not Lakyn." Her tone is almost accusing, as if I've been trying to hide the fact from her and for the first time since ending up on the Holy Grounds, I feel hurt.

"Right," I mumble, shifting uncomfortably in my chair. I don't know what I just said to make her realize that, but I wish I had said it sooner.

"But if you're not him, then who are you?" Her brow furrows in confusion, and her eyes that are normally so bright with wisdom are now clouded in suspicion. I feel like a traitor in a foreign land and that's usually accompanied by an execution.

How many languages do I have to say this in? Do they have their own?

"I'm the son of Lakyn Meyer. My name is Aftyn."

It's slight, but I can see her shoulders shaking a little since I'm sitting right beside her. She's… laughing? But why?

"Lakyn knocked someone up?" she asks loudly, doubling over with laughter.

The way she howls, clutching her belly… this doesn't sound like her at all and it's more than a bit unnerving. So much so, that Luminescence suddenly appears out of nowhere and places a wooden chalice filled with Cactus of Ambrosia to The Daughter's lips. She stays with her until the drink is gone, swallowed down and resting in her belly.

And just like that, the laughter has waned into that tranquil smile and the world seems to shine through her eyes again.

It makes me wonder now, as Sun Wolf approaches me with a chalice of my very own, if The Daughter is actually in charge here or if she's nothing more than a false god they're keeping hostage.

Kind of like Pop's 'roommate.'

FOUR

Old Habits

DAPHNE

I'm lying in the tent one of these psychos gave me, staring at the faded blue fabric above my head, and even though I know it's not that cool out here in the daytime, I can't stop shivering. This ratty old sleeping bag has probably been around longer than I have, but at least it's something, and it's thick enough to wrap up in when the chills rush over my skin until my teeth chatter.

Fuck, I feel like shit.

My leg is itching again, and I try to rub at it through my pants. Scratching will only tear the makeshift bandage away again, and I need to keep this one on as long as I can. These light weaver people are unstable, but at least

35

they've tried to help me. No one has tried to touch me or hurt me—unless you count offering me that toxic shit from the cacti around here. It's the drug of choice for each of them, but all it does is make them high as fuck and batshit crazy.

Still, drug addicts or not, they've been decent. One of them gave me some expired antibiotics, another used some desert version of moonshine to try and clean my leg, and a few of the women have helped me make some bandages out of old clothes.

It's honestly the only reason I haven't slit one of their throats yet.

Why did you leave me here, Lakyn?

The memory of him driving away floods me again, making my chest ache as I remember the way the dust pelted my skin. Watching the taillights from the SUV disappear into the distance is the most alone I've ever felt.

I don't know what I did wrong. He told me to get ready to act on his word, and I walked as fast as I could back to the truck to get my backpack. I'd even made sure my largest knife was ready to grab as soon as he gave me a sign, but before I'd even made it back to the center of the commune Lakyn had stormed past me.

I'd called out to him. I'd *screamed* his name when I saw him going for the truck, but when I'd tried to run after him... my leg gave out. All I'd got in response was a face full of dirt as his tires spun before finally launching him down their excuse for a road. No glance back at me, no wave, no acknowledgement that he'd heard me at all.

The pain in my chest twists again and I can hear the whine slipping through my clenched teeth as I shiver in the sleeping bag. I hate feeling so weak. I shouldn't even be thinking like this. I've never needed anyone but myself. Hell, I've never even *wanted* anyone around me, never cared about anyone's opinion of me before. Never cared if someone stayed in my life.

But I've never met someone like Lakyn Meyer before.

He's... everything I always wanted to be. Completely honest. Free. He never puts on a mask to make society accept him. No, instead he kicks in the doors of civility that society tries to construct in front of him and flashes that grin whenever the world questions him. He owes allegiance to no one, apologizes to no one, and once upon a time he'd wanted me to join him on that journey.

Until we found Beatrix.

It hadn't taken me long to connect the dots, or, rather, the blonde hair on the crazy bitch's head to the painting that Lakyn had mangled in the basement of that Satanic church. I should have realized it sooner, but the way Lakyn had talked about Beatrix when he was telling Aftyn stories had seemed so positive. It wasn't until I saw them standing across from each other that Lakyn's hate for her was clear.

He wanted her dead.

For a moment I think he even wanted *me* to do it, which I would have done gladly… but then he left.

He left me here with these crazy fucks, and his stupid kid, and the bitch he hates, and I still don't know why. That question keeps me up at night when the chills or my fucking leg won't let me sleep. *Why leave me behind? Why drive away? Why not wait for me to bring back a knife so we could kill her together?*

It just doesn't make sense.

I've thought about killing her and finishing the job he'd clearly wanted me to do before he left, but Aftyn is always with her and I don't know if Lakyn wants him dead yet.

If Lakyn was here I'd know what to do. I'd know the right steps to take to fix whatever I did wrong that made him leave me here in this miserable, cheery version of Hell. If Lakyn was here maybe my mind wouldn't feel so damn fuzzy and distorted.

"How are you feeling today, Little Star?" one of the idiots asks, leaning into my tent. "I brought you breakfast."

I lift my head to look at her and the sorry excuse for food on the clay plate in her hands. When I see it's the same shit they eat for every meal, I drop my head back onto my arm. That's not fucking breakfast. Breakfast includes foods like eggs, or pancakes, but this bitch doesn't have any of that. She has slimy cactus and beans, which makes my stomach churn just thinking about tasting again.

I hate this place, I hate their excuse for food, and I hate how sugar-coated and happy everyone acts all the time. Wrapping my hate around me like a warm blanket, I shift deeper into the sleeping bag and don't bother talking to her, but even after she sets the plate down… her shadow doesn't move.

"You look pale, Little Star. You should let The Daughter tend to your wound. Her Light can heal all things, and with the gift of the Cactus, you will feel much better. I can bring you—"

"No." Pulling the sleeping bag over my head, I hear her sigh, followed by the rustle of the tent flap as she finally leaves me alone again. It's the same woman who helped me bandage my leg last time, and while I needed the fabric from her to keep my leg from oozing all over my clothes, I don't want to be her friend.

I don't want to be here at all.

But, as much as I hate to admit it, I'm not going to be able to move tomorrow if I don't put *something* in my stomach—even if it's disgusting.

Sitting up, I pull the jacket tighter around me and drag the plate of boiled cactus and mostly uncooked beans toward me. The jug of water from the well that one of the guys with a crazy name got for me is the only way I manage to get the beans down, swallowing them like pills. I know I need the protein, and the energy, but the beans are easy by comparison. The only way to get the cactus down is to chew it, which is pretty disgusting. It's not the flavor, which is vaguely citrusy, it's the fucking texture. There's a slime to it that makes me want to gag every time I have to force it down and I don't know how any of the crazies here handle it.

Probably because they're high as fuck.

The chime of bells echoing across the commune tells me that the workday has started for the 'Children of Light' and the only thing I'm grateful for is that they've mostly left me alone. Hell, even Aftyn seems to have forgotten about his plan to murder me for killing Willa.

Of course, he jumped at the chance to drink that cactus shit and hop into bed with Beatrix —*The Daughter*. Now he's just as crazy as the rest of them.

Such fucking bullshit.

My bladder nudges me, and I get out of the sleeping bag and put on my shoes, wincing at the throbbing ache in my thigh. I'm getting used to it, but it's the worst in the morning when I haven't grown as numb to the pain as I am after I'm up for a while. It almost makes their cactus drink tempting, but I have no interest in joining their fake happy tribe of hippies.

I'd rather be in pain than witless.

Grabbing the plate, I head toward the communal dining area. It's nothing fancy, just rows of tables set up under canopies to keep the sun off everyone, which I'm sure is brutal in the dead of summer... not that I plan to be here by then. The bright morning sun makes everything shimmer, and I can tell I'm not walking as straight as I should be, but it's not easy when I feel like hell and the ground keeps tilting in funny ways.

"Ah, young one, did you enjoy the gifts of the Earth?" An older woman smiles at me as she takes the plate from my hands, but I don't return the look. Being with Lakyn was supposed to make it so I never had to wear my mask again, and I don't want to put it back on.

I miss him.

Although, right now, I miss real toilets more. These fucked-up composting toilets are like something from a hippie's nightmare, and the stench is horrible, but I manage to hold my breath until I'm done and I'm able to stumble back toward my tent.

I may be trapped in the land of shiny, happy people wearing their perfect, smiling masks, but at least I've got my own space to retreat to. I've still got my backpack.

Another chill has me shivering as I stand outside my tent, watching the psychos wander around, but my gaze ends up focusing on the worn track where I last saw Lakyn driving away. He's somewhere out there. Probably back at his home in Mesa.

Wait.

Even though all I want to do is lay back down, I feel an idea clicking to life and with it comes a shaky plan. It's not perfect, but my life never has been, and I've always managed to survive. Heading toward the small cluster of adobe houses, I aim directly for the one where Aftyn has been holed up with Beatrix since Lakyn left us here. I can hear them fucking before I even reach the door, but I didn't expect anything else. That's all they do.

Get high.

Spout insane shit.

Fuck.

Repeat.

The old hinges creak, but the grunts and moans don't stutter, and I look around at the tables and cabinets in the front space. Being as quiet as I can, I dig through the drawers and shelves, moving stuff gently to avoid getting caught.

I'm about to give up when I see a small bookshelf tucked in the corner and the little rectangle I've been searching for is resting on the middle shelf.

Aftyn's phone.

Smiling to myself, I feel my lip split, but I just lick the blood away as I pocket the device and head back out the door. I can feel how dizzy I am while I make it back to the tent, but I push my weakness aside and pack my backpack quickly, refilling my water bottles from the jug. The phone isn't charged, but I know what's on it. Lakyn's address is in one of those text messages, and I saw Aftyn enter his code into the phone more than once on our little road trip.

I don't have to stay here.

There's a way out of this hell and back to Lakyn, and if I can make it back to him on my own maybe that will finally prove to him that I'm committed.

I won't forget him like Beatrix.

I won't hate him like Aftyn.

If he'll let me, I'll be whatever he wants me to be just for the chance to be with someone that doesn't expect me to wear a mask.

Someone who wants me for who I really am, who wants me to be a part of their family *because* of who I am… and I want that more than anything.

———

I'VE BEEN WALKING for a long time. Away from the decorated cacti on the roadside, back toward civilization. A few cars have passed me, but no one has even slowed down yet, and I'm not sure how long I can keep moving.

Thinking about it isn't helping though.

I just need to put one foot in front of the other. Again and again.

A horn blaring makes me jump, and I try to step onto the shoulder, but my leg gives out and I hit the dirt hard, scratching my hands on the rocks and bruising my knees.

"Fuck," I groan, trying to summon the strength to stand again.

Then I hear someone shouting.

Lifting my head, I see a man jogging toward me. The car is pulled to the side of the road, and I think there's a woman standing beside it on the passenger side, but it's hard to tell from this distance.

What's he saying?

"—kay?" He's panting as he comes closer, leaning on his knees to look down at me. "Hey, are you okay?"

"No." I shake my head, and even though I told myself I wouldn't put my mask back on, I'll do whatever it takes to get back to Lakyn. Turning the tears on is easy, like flexing a muscle I haven't used in a while, and when he sees me crying his face softens.

"Shit, I'm so sorry. We were trying to see if you needed a ride, I didn't mean to scare you." Stepping forward, he takes my arm gently and helps me stand. "God, you look like a kid. How old are you? Why are you out here in the middle of nowhere?"

"M-my boyfriend convinced me to come out here to this place, but it was a cult. They're j-just a cult, and I wanted to go home, but he wouldn't leave with me and I don't have a c-car." I add a sniffle, wiping at the tears I've managed to summon, and he coos with concern as he helps me back to the car.

"Is she okay?" the woman calls out, shading her eyes against the sun.

"I think she's just scratched up," he answers as we get closer, and I can see they're both older. Closer to the age of that couple Lakyn and I killed for being so rude, but as long as they're nice I won't carve out one of their hearts. I've been hitchhiking for a while now and my instincts are usually pretty good, so I think these two will just help me.

"Oh, sweetheart... how long have you been out here?" The woman opens the back door, shoving things to the side so I can get in, and I drop into the seat with a wince that isn't faked. My leg is throbbing and itching, but if I tell them about that they might take me to a hospital instead of Lakyn's.

"She got involved in some cult," the man, who I think is her husband, answers for me.

"Seriously? That's crazy."

"Yeah. Let's get back in the car, Sharon. We should get moving again so we don't get hit."

He shuts my door and waves at his wife, and a moment later they're in their seats and I can feel the air conditioning. It makes me shiver, but I don't complain. This is infinitely better than dying on the side of the road.

Before they can ask me questions that I'll have to make up lies for, I dig out Aftyn's phone and hold it out. "Do you have a charger for this?"

"Sure, sweetheart! I've got the same one," Sharon replies, taking it from me, and I assume she's plugging it in. "Are you hungry?"

I nod when she glances back at me, and a minute later I've got a bottle of Coke and a protein bar in my hands, devouring them both as I offer them a sob story that has them making little noises of shock and sadness. Naive young girl follows her boyfriend on a vacation into the desert, accidentally joins a cult, realizes it's terrible, and just wants to get back to her family. To her uncle's house outside of Phoenix. A few more tears and the two of them are intent on helping me get 'home.'

Unfortunately, Dan and Sharon aren't going that far, but they promise to get me as close as they can, and as I hug my backpack and lean against the window to sleep, I can hear them talking about buying me a bus ticket.

That's more than enough generosity for me to let them live.

Killing them for their car might get me to Lakyn faster, but I don't completely trust my ability to drive right now, so if I can get a bus ticket to Mesa—and sleep on the way—I'll fucking take it.

After all, as soon as I get back to Lakyn, everything will be better.

Then I can take my mask off for good.

FIVE

It's A Good Life

THE DAUGHTER

My body is slick with sweat, but so is his. The warmth of his breath against my lips when he lets out one last euphoric groan as I feel him spill his seed inside me makes me shiver.

While I have no intention of dying, I'll need an heir if the Light calls me home. Someone that will carry on the good work that I've done here and continue to bring others toward the truth.

I place a hand on either side of his face as he leans down the last inch and presses his lips to mine. When his curve up into a smile, I shake my head fondly and give him a gentle push away.

He's very dutiful in his tasks, loyal to the point

of no return already, and as he lays down behind me and presses his body against mine, I know that any child that we may produce will be the greatest Light Weaver that existence will ever know.

He brushes my hair aside so that he can rest his chin on my bare shoulder, and I interlink my fingers with his once his arm is wrapped securely around my waist.

This life is so wonderfully strange sometimes… the son of my enemy is now the man that I choose in this life and the next.

Who would have thought that Lakyn would have been able to produce something good with his miserable life? Something so pure that has never harmed another or harbored the same thoughts of ill repute as the one that had a hand in making him?

A few moments later, his breathing is even. Being the One True Soul Lover of Light takes a lot out of him, but once he's well rested, we'll take another meal, share ideologies, and consummate our relationship again.

I feel a little tired myself, but I can't stop thinking about Lakyn for some reason. I had not thought of him in so long, but to think that I hadn't recognized him as easily as I saw his mirror image in the boy makes me wonder if the Cactus of Ambrosia is running dry faster than it should.

Sun Wolf, Raindrop, and Luminescence will find a newer, sturdier supplier of the Water. I'll separate them and send them into the furthest regions of the Holy Grounds of Light until it's done, and all will be well again.

My vision will be true again, and come with the perfect clarity of the Light that seems to have waned and allowed me to harbor such confusion.

When I first saw Aftyn, I'd been sure it was Lakyn. His name had appeared in my mind like a bubble rising to the surface, and at first I'd only remembered a sense of loyalty. To me. Once upon a time he'd followed me, but then he turned away. I remember the anger in him now, that simmering rage that I saw in him when I did not recognize him as he stood before me, instead looking only at his son.

A soft sigh escapes me because as I remember that moment, another irksome thought rises.

Lakyn kept saying the name of a man I don't recall. One that he repeated with such insistence that I wonder if this unknown person should hold some meaning for me.

What was the name?

I close my eyes for a moment and wrack my brain, but as any memory I should supposedly have of this person, the name itself eludes me. Lakyn and the other are part of a past blocked out by the Light.

When the boy awakens, I'll ask him about this mysterious shadow from my past and hope that he can shed some light on an otherwise forgotten subject. Perhaps it will be the key to unlocking Lakyn's anger so he can finally be free of it.

I ALWAYS LOVE the way the greenhouse smells after a midday nap. As I slowly make my way down the first aisle, I notice that the beans are sprouting nicely. Running my fingers along the edge of the table, I continue my examination of what we've been able to accomplish with love and Light alone.

A glance over my shoulder to ensure that I'm alone spurs me on and I move quickly, my feet becoming one with the wet dirt that coats the floors inside. A sharp left at the end of the aisle and I remove a false panel that allows me to climb down a ladder into another, smaller room that even my closest Weavers aren't aware of. Taking a deep breath, I follow the underground path for about ten minutes until I find the next entrance.

I run a hand along the wall next to it, blindly since it's completely dark where I am now, and when I find what I'm looking for, I quickly move my fingers in the Way of the Light to open the door.

Stepping into the room, I carefully move toward the center table, guided only by memorizing the number of footsteps needed to find it, then light the lantern that sits in the middle. As the flame flares to life, the room becomes dimly lit. The air hangs much lower here, and the drawings on the walls were made by someone that I was a long time ago.

I sometimes make my way down here when I want to remind myself that I'm a better person now. That teaching the Way of the Light to so many confirms that the girl I once was died alongside whatever memories have been prodding at me, fighting to force their way back ever since Lakyn found me here.

But much like the air below the Holy Ground of Light, the shell of my former self still clings desperately to the secrets I hide here.

She wants to be free again, to roam the Earth as she once did, though I do my best to forget her a little more each time I slip away from my children to seek out this place where she haunts me relentlessly.

I want her to go away.

I want her to die.

Slowly, painfully, in a way that she'll never try to harm me again by trying to make me remember who I was.

Trixie; that's what Lakyn called me. That's the name he shouted at me, the one that was supposed to make the ghost of the girl that hides in this room rise from the grave where I've been trying to bury the remnants.

I splay the palms of my hands on the table, my body hunching over as I tell myself that all will be well.

I have the one thing that Lakyn always wanted and he won't come back again. He sees that I am, and always have been, better than him, and that put such a chink in his armor that only madness would drive him back to me.

Stop.

I blink rapidly a few times, feeling the pressure of those hidden memories pushing at the inside of my mind again.

I have to get out of this room.

It's too dangerous to linger here. She's becoming stronger, regaining her bearings, and if I'm not careful… she'll take over me again.

"Daughter?"

I gasp loudly as Aftyn's voice breaks my focus. Leaning forward, I quickly blow out the lone flame in the lantern and turn around to peer at the darkened room where I know he's waiting.

I can only hope he didn't see the insane scrawlings on the walls as I listen to the uncertain shuffling of footsteps as they make their way toward me, then the gentle *thump* of a body colliding with mine.

"Sorry," he says with a nervous laugh. "It's kind of dark in here."

"You shouldn't be in here," I reply quietly as I take his hand and lead him out of the room.

And neither should I.

"SHE'S GONE?" I ask Sun Wolf in surprise. *What could have possibly driven Little Star away from us?* Anyone that joins us always feels loved, cared about, taken care of, and never wants to return to their former lives.

"Yes, I'm sorry. We only just noticed an hour ago," he replies quietly as he lowers his eyes to the ground.

I reach forward and place a hand on his shoulder, giving it a reassuring squeeze. "Feel no shame. She was not yours to watch. Little

Star came to us of her own free will and used the same to return to her life. It's always been allowed, and you know this better than anyone."

He nods, but I can see that he doesn't know if he'll be punished. However, what has happened does not warrant punishment. It should be rewarded because with Little Star gone, Aftyn will rapidly lose memories of his former self and surrender to the Light completely.

"I have a request of you, my friend," I begin with a small smile. Sun Wolf raises his eyes from the ground to mine and when he sees no anger in me, I can see the relief wash over him almost instantly.

"Speak it and see it done," he responds eagerly.

"Find Raindrop and Luminescence. I need the three of you to spread out on the Holy Grounds. There is a new Cactus of Ambrosia springing somewhere in the vastness of the love we've built here, and it must be brought to replace the one that's dying."

He straightens his shoulders, nods at me, and smiles at Aftyn before he turns around and goes dutifully to complete the mission I've charged him with.

When he returns, I'll drink from the new spring and all will be well again.

It'll make the old girl hidden beneath the Holy Ground finally die and I'll never have a need to go into that room again.

SIX

Homecoming

DAPHNE

"Turn left here," I say, pointing out the windshield as my eyes switch between the map on the phone and the road in front of me.

This is it.

I recognize the neighborhood, and my skin feels electric as I get closer and closer to Lakyn.

"I'm glad your uncle lives in a safe neighborhood. A girl like you needs to be more careful," the man in the driver seat chastises.

"I know," I reply absentmindedly, focusing on the way our little dot is moving steadily toward the address that feels like home.

"I mean it, Bethany. You can't just hitchhike around. There are dangerous people in this world," he continues, using the fake name I gave him, and I force a sweet smile. He's one of the decent ones, which I'm grateful for because I don't have the energy to deal with one of the bad ones right now. His opinions won't matter soon anyway.

I just need to pacify him and get to Lakyn.

"I promise I won't do it again. I just needed to get to my uncle, and I didn't have any money." I sit up straight and jab my finger toward the next turn even though the sudden movement makes my thigh throb. "Here! Turn here, this is his street!"

"Okay, what's the number?" he asks, looking toward the phone, and I let him see the screen. We're both scanning the house numbers, but a second later I don't need to. I can see Willa's SUV in the driveway, and I remember the front of Lakyn's house clearly.

"There," I whisper, pointing to it, and the man pulls up to the curb. My stomach tightens, and I lick at my dry lips as I stare out the driver-side window at the front door.

"Okay." The man throws the truck into 'park' and twists to look at me. "Ready to tell me why he didn't pick you up at the bus station, Bethany?" When he uses my fake name again, it takes me a second to process his question, but I've been lying for so long that even with my head tired and fuzzy I manage to come up with a plausible answer.

"I tried his number before I left my boyfriend, but it belongs to someone else. I don't know his new one."

"Then how do you know he lives here?" This old guy is tense, protective, and I almost want to laugh. He has no idea who I am, or what I'm capable of, or what I would have done to him if he hadn't been a decent man.

Time to lie again.

"That's his car," I answer, pointing at the SUV as I pull my backpack into my lap and turn on my sweet voice. "Thank you so much for the ride. You absolutely saved my life."

"No need to thank me," he says, glancing at the truck before he looks at me kindly, his dusky green eyes creasing at the corners with his smile. "You actually remind me of my daughter when she was your age. I hope that if she was ever in need of help, someone good would stop and help her too." Sighing, he turns back to the house and then faces me again. "I'll wait here to make sure he's home and you get inside. Stay safe, Bethany, and ask your uncle to take you to a doctor. You don't look well, and I really do think you're getting sick. Promise me, okay?"

"I will. Promise." Nodding, I open the door and get out, clenching my teeth hard to keep from making a noise when I put weight on my leg again. It's always worse at first, but I can handle it. I can handle anything now that I'm this close to Lakyn.

I wave at the man as I head up the walk to the front door, swallowing as a strange, nervous energy fills me up. Being near Lakyn Meyer makes me feel so many things I'm not used to feeling, and I have no idea how to process them. All I know is that I need to be here, with him.

I'm *meant* to be here.

I take a deep breath and ring the doorbell before adjusting the straps of my backpack and shifting my weight to my good leg. When I don't hear anything, I try to finger comb my hair, quickly straighten my shirt, then knock.

This time I heard a voice inside, a male voice, and I'm pretty sure it was Lakyn's, but it was too far away to make out. Just as I'm preparing to knock again, the door opens, and Ichabod's expression shifts from annoyed to surprised before his eyes wander past me.

"What are you doing here?" he finally asks when his gaze returns to mine.

"I came back."

"I can see that. *Why* did you come back here?" Ichabod sounds sincerely confused, his brows pulling together slightly, and I hate that I can't see into the house to tell if Lakyn is home.

"Everything okay?" The man in the truck calls out through his open window and I turn to wave at him.

"Just fine! Thank you again!" I shout back before turning to Ichabod and lowering my voice. "Just let me in so he'll go away. Please."

"Fuck. Fine," Ichabod grumbles, stepping back and holding the door open as he gestures inside with an exasperated sigh.

"Thanks," I mumble and catch him waving to the man who gave me the ride as I move inside. The door shuts behind me and that tingly feeling has my skin humming and my teeth buzzing. I take a step toward the living room, hoping to see Lakyn, *needing* to see him, but my fucking leg chooses that moment to give out and I end up barely catching myself against a small table covered in mail.

"Shit, are you okay?" Ichabod wraps a surprisingly firm grip around my arm, and I'm so tempted to shake him off because I want to face Lakyn standing upright, strong, but I don't know if I can actually manage that right now.

"I'll be fine. Is Lakyn here?" I ask, glancing at Ichabod. All of the surprise and concern melts away and he suddenly looks incredibly serious, almost sad, but the expression fades when he adjusts his hold on my arm and helps me stand up straight.

"Yeah," he answers curtly. "He's here, but you're definitely not fine." Ichabod mutters a few curses under his breath and leads me into the living room—which is disappointingly empty. I can smell cigarette smoke on the air and I'm pretty sure Ichabod doesn't smoke. At least, I didn't see him smoke during the short time I was here last, but he said Lakyn is here and I don't think he'd lie about that. He stops me by the couch and nudges me toward it. "Sit down, Daphne."

"Wait." I try to push backward, fighting his grip. "I want to see Lakyn first."

"You need to sit down so I can look at your leg."

"It's fine, can you just— *fuck*!" My leg buckles completely, a vicious spike of pain making my head pound and my stomach churn, and it's only Ichabod's fierce hold on my arm and a sharp shove that gets me on the couch instead of the floor.

But if he hadn't hit my goddamn thigh, it wouldn't have happened at all.

Hissing air through my teeth, I glare up at him and snarl, "What the fuck!"

"See? You're not fine," Ichabod replies, deadpan and completely unconcerned as he points at me. "Stay here. Don't touch anything. I'll get the first aid stuff."

"But I want—"

"To see Lakyn. I know." Rolling his eyes, Ichabod steps back and crosses his arms, then he just stares. Right at me, with his jaw twitching from how hard he has it clenched.

For a second I'm worried he's going to toss me out in a fit of jealousy, but if he thinks I'll let him do that before I see Lakyn, he's fucking delusional. However, threatening him won't help me right now, especially since Ichabod seems to be blurring at the edges in a way that's definitely not natural. Plus, *you catch more flies with honey*, and all that bullshit. Taking a breath, I try to look meek, sad, and not in pain. "Please, Ichabod?"

"Goddammit." Huffing, he gestures down the hall. "He's sleeping right now and waking him up would be a really fucking bad idea for both of us. So, why don't you just let me look at that leg and we can both wait for him to get up in his own time."

"Okay," I relent and force a small smile. *Just be polite.* "Thank you."

"Sure," he mumbles before heading out of the living room.

I listen to the quiet of the house for a minute, straining my ears to see if I can catch a hint of Lakyn's voice… but there's nothing. Just the distant sound of a cabinet shutting from down the hall. Shifting on the couch, I take off my backpack and set it beside me, reaching in to make sure one of my knives is just inside the opening.

Ichabod might be sincere about helping with my leg, but there's no way he's forgotten that I'm competition. He heard Lakyn ask me to be a part of his family, he knows that I already killed Willa to stay, and there's always a chance he'll try to take me out before Lakyn wakes up.

"YOU'VE GOT A FEVER, DAPHNE," Ichabod insists, but I just roll my eyes as he continues wrapping gauze around the cut.

It looks a lot worse than the last time I paid attention to it. I've been keeping it wrapped up, trying to keep it clean, or at least the assholes at Camp Desert Kumbaya have, but it doesn't seem to be helping. The cut is wider than it used to be, and the skin around it is swollen and bright red. The actual cut is the problem though, and the sight of it is what flipped Ichabod from irritated and annoyed to freaking out as soon as I rolled the yoga pants down.

I think he's overreacting, but I do have to admit it looks bad. It's oozing and doesn't seem to be healing even though it's been about two weeks since Aftyn took the cheap shot at me. Of course, it probably looks even redder than usual because Ichabod has been fucking around with it for what feels like hours, which is making me feel ten times worse than I did when I walked in.

"Take these," Ichabod says in a gruff voice, tossing a bottle of pills into my lap, and I turn them over to see they're pain relievers.

"It doesn't hurt that much. I'll be fine."

"Just fucking take them," he snaps, taping off the gauze as he grits his teeth again.

"Why?" I ask, opening the bottle to look at the pills. I'm not sure what this brand of pain reliever is supposed to look like, but I'm not just taking random fucking pills from someone who has a good reason to see me dead.

"Jesus Christ, Daphne. If I had a thermometer here, I'd be able to prove that you have a fever, probably a pretty serious one, but for now you just need to listen to me." Ichabod scrubs at his face before he looks up at me again from where he's sitting on the floor. "I did my best to clean that up, but it's a mess. I'd tell you to go to a fucking hospital, but "

"No way," I interrupt, and he groans, leaning back on his hands to stare at me.

"Exactly. I knew you wouldn't go even if I suggested it, but that's definitely infected and it's not going to heal without serious antibiotics and some stitches. Neither of which I have here."

"I'll be fine," I repeat for the hundredth time, but for the first time I'm concerned I might be wrong. I think it's because of how cold Ichabod's fingers felt on my skin, and the sincere look of concern mixed with horror when he saw my leg. Also, the fact that a few times when I looked at him there were two Ichabods instead of one, which is never a good sign when it comes to health. Physical or mental.

Thinking about it makes me dig out the water bottle from the side of my bag and I toss back three of the pills. If this is how Ichabod plans to kill me, at least I'll be in Lakyn's house where I belong when I die… but something makes me trust him.

For now, anyway.

"Did Lakyn do that to you?" he whispers, and I almost choke on the water in my effort to defend him.

"No! It was fucking Aftyn. He was pissed because I killed Willa."

"Did you…" Ichabod starts to ask the million-dollar question, and I can't help but laugh a little.

"Did I kill him? No. He's too busy getting high and fucking the queen of the desert for me to waste my time on him."

"What?" Lakyn's gruff voice makes me spin around, but the throb of pain in my leg is a distant pain when I set my eyes on him. He's shirtless, wearing a pair of comfortable pants, and running a hand over his face as he walks into the living room.

"You're up," Ichabod says, scrambling up from the floor, and Lakyn grins in the most perfect way.

"Obviously." He snags his cigarettes and a lighter from the table before dropping into the chair he commanded the room from the last time we were here. "And apparently you picked up a stray while I was napping."

"She just showed up," Ichabod replies, shoving his hands into his pockets, but Lakyn just lights the cigarette and takes a long puff, letting out a stream of smoke in our direction.

"I didn't want to be there anymore," I explain, trying to make my voice sound cool and confident, even though I don't feel either of those things at the moment. Still, just the sight of Lakyn fills me with an energy that I've been missing the last two weeks. It's like the sun has returned to my universe, like my center is back and I know my place once more. Licking my dry lips, I set my water bottle aside and lean forward. "I wanted to be with you."

Lakyn chuckles, staring at me through the haze of smoke. "Why?"

"Because I—" Words escape me, flittering away as I stare at him, and I know I should remember all the things I planned to say. I practiced everything I wanted to say so many times in my mind, rehearsing it on the bus and in cars, but facing off with Lakyn Meyer seems to make all of those planned words disappear in the shimmery buzzing I can see in the air.

"Jinkies, Red." Rolling his eyes, Lakyn puffs a few smoke rings toward the ceiling. "You made it all the way back here and you can't even tell me what the fuck you and Ichabod were gossiping about?"

He doesn't know.

I feel a smile slide over my lips and despite the pounding ache in my thigh, I adjust myself to sit up tall. I want to look strong, in control. I want to remind Lakyn why he wanted me to be a part of his family. "I got bored listening to Aftyn and Beatrix fucking each other all the time, and I really hate that hippie shit."

Lakyn's jaw goes rigid, tense, and I feel my own body stiffen in response. Hell, even Ichabod looks like he's trying to disappear into thin air as Lakyn lets his cigarette dangle while he sits up in the chair and narrows his eyes at me. After a moment, his voice comes out too calm and quiet as he asks, "Aftyn and Beatrix are fucking?"

SEVEN

Trix Aren't For Kids

LAKYN

Red swallows the lump in her throat and I can see that she's getting a little nervous at having dropped this bomb on me.

Maybe she thought it would be a good idea to rile me up, and maybe somewhere in that fucked up brain of hers she thought I'd drop everything I ever knew and tell her that all I would ever need is her.

Yeah, right, I think with an eye roll as I clear my throat and attempt to regain my composure.

So, the kid is fucking Trixie and they think it's okay. She's probably got him smacked up too—of course she does, she wouldn't know how to treat him otherwise.

"Are you sure?" I ask, pulling the cigarette from my lips and blowing out a puff of smoke.

"I'm not dumb, Lakyn," she replies stubbornly. "I know what fucking sounds like."

I chuckle.

I'm sure she means she had that knowledge *before* the little show we put on for her, but I've already disappointed Ichabod enough and the last thing he needs to find out is that I slipped for sure. He's been pestering me about that satanic princess he found in the SUV for the last two weeks and I'm fucking over it. Although, considering I didn't go for the pussy, I don't think it should count.

Either way, I don't want to deal with the fall out of another emotional breakdown. When I didn't have Trixie in tow he full-blown lost it, and it took a couple of days of me fucking him hard for Ichabod to get his heart back into it. So, if Red tries to talk about our little party favor, I'll just slit her throat and be done with it, cause I'm not putting up with *that* again.

Just like I have no plans of tolerating the kid fucking my new least favorite druggie blonde.

"Alright, so the boy and the bitch think they can just fuck each other out in the desert with no consequences." Sucking my teeth, I watch the ash fall off the end of my cigarette before I lift it for another drag.

Decision made.

"Guess that means I gotta head back to the Holy Land of Bullshit and break that up," I finally say as I let out a breath.

"Wait a minute." Ichabod's tone is stern, and I grit my teeth. When I got home, I understood his bitchfest. I let him down, I admitted it, and I was hoping that maybe his balls would have retreated over the last two weeks, but I see that I'm wrong.

"What?" I bark as I turn to glare at him.

"Why do you care if Trixie fucks Aftyn?"

I rub my forehead with my thumb and turn my eyes away for a moment. It's that same fucking look he gave me when I manhandled him back into the house after I got back. The one that's accusing me of being a liar and of not being able to keep my promises.

"Lakyn," he says, his tone matching his eyes. "Why do you care?"

A grin slips across my lips and settles on half of my face as I take another drag from my smoke. I look Ichabod up and down for a moment before I shrug. "You've known Beatrix almost as long as I have. We both know she's a festering bitch and the last thing I need is for her to turn the kid into one too."

"Is that the only reason?" he persists as he crosses his arms over his chest and juts his chin out.

"What the fuck is this? An interrogation? I don't want that bitch giving the kid a disease. Maybe it's the *daddy* in me that you were so desperate to drag out finally showing up," I say snidely. "Isn't that why you did this? To see if I would give a fuck about someone other than myself for once? Or maybe you wanted to see if it would slow me down knowing that some rogue spunk made its way to a random fuck in Vegas and have it show up at my front door. Not a chance in Hell, *Ichy, baby*."

His arms drop from his chest and all the macho bravado that I know he's been nurturing the last couple of weeks seems to slip away in the next breath he lets out.

"Besides…" I say as I reach over and flick ashes into the ashtray he hasn't broken. "I thought you wanted to see your bestie?"

His eyes light up slightly and I can see the hope shining brightly.

"You mean—"

"No." I wave a hand, cutting him off immediately. "I promised that I'd bring her back, and I will, but you have to promise to be a good boy and give me time to go talk some reason into them, mkay?"

Red shudders. I catch it out of the corner of my eye, and I arch an eyebrow at her curiously. She looks like she's trembling and when she wraps her arms around herself, all I can envision is her blowing chunks all over my fucking carpet.

"Did you get on that cactus shit too while you were out there?" I ask, and she shakes her head.

"No. I refused to drink that stuff."

"Huh…" I tilt my head looking her over, and while she definitely *could* be dealing with withdrawal, I don't think she'd lie to me. She's too damn in love with me. "You sick?"

"I'm fine," she answers almost immediately, giving me those puppy dog eyes and it takes everything in me not to kick her and leave her behind just so she doesn't throw up in the car.

"Well, just remember that good girls swallow," I tell her with a wink. Ichabod scowls when she looks at me with those fucking stars in her eyes, but he doesn't have anything to worry about.

Honestly, at this point in my life, I'd hate to have to break in a new hole. Besides, he knows what I like, and he lets me take it whenever I want.

Turning back to Ichabod, I flash him a grin. "So, you gonna stay and be a good boy?"

"I suppose," he finally relents.

"Excellent! Now I'm gonna get dressed"—I pause long enough to jab out the cigarette in the ashtray—"then we're gonna get out of here and I'll be back before you know it."

"With Bea?" he asks quietly as I walk by him.

"As promised," I reply with a wink and march out of the room.

The grin instantly drops from my face and I'm doing my best to keep my steps steady. This bitch always likes to overstep her boundaries, but this time she's gone too fucking far.

I could care less that she's letting someone else stick their dick in her rotten hole, or that it's my useless kid. No, what's got my eyes set to kill is that this bitch doesn't remember the one person that loves her more than she deserves because she's too busy becoming a druggie guru to some fuckwads in the desert and *that* is something neither of them deserve to enjoy.

Nothing a little walk down memory lane won't be able to fix, I think to myself as I disappear into my bedroom and slam the door shut behind me.

"ALRIGHT, let's get on the road again, Red," I call out when I walk back into the little love circle that she and Ichabod have formed.

"Okay." She twists on the couch to look up at me and nods before awkwardly standing. I'm pretty sure she sways, unsteady on her feet, and I catch the way Ichabod almost reaches for her. They were whispering about something when I walked in, but I really don't give a shit what it is. Ichabod knows his place, and Red would do just about anything I half-suggested to her. As long as stays upright anyway, because now that I'm actually paying attention to her, she looks pale as a sheet.

"Well?" I prompt her and Ichabod sighs at me like he actually cares about this murderous little street urchin. Of course, he's always had a soft spot for the particularly unhinged ones.

"I'll go get in the car," Red mumbles, throwing her backpack over her shoulder and swaying slightly as she walks out the front door. I really don't give a fuck if she's drunk or sick. She's just going to bear witness, so as long as she stays conscious I'll keep her around.

"Wait, Lakyn?" Ichabod pipes up, his voice small.

I do my best not to sigh as I look down at his skinny little hand on my arm.

"What now?" I ask as calmly as I can.

"That girl in the back seat…"

"Hm?"

I have no idea who the hell he's talking about for a second and then it clicks—*oh! The new goat girl. Right.* He's been obsessed with that bitch since the night I got back even though she's been liquified for a while now and off my radar for even longer.

"What about her?" I ask impatiently.

"Please tell me the truth, Lakyn… Did you fuck her?" he asks me quietly.

"You've really got your priorities screwed up, Ichabod," I scoff as I shake my head and walk out the door. I almost make it to the car when I hear his whiny little voice crack behind me.

"Did you?"

Grabbing the handle, I pull the driver's side open and look over at where he's standing in the doorway. "Technically? No."

"What does that mean?" he calls out and I slip into the driver's seat. I slam the car door as Red begins to secure her seatbelt, crank the key, then roll down the window.

"I'll be back with your bestie in a few hours. Don't wait up, sweetheart!" I shout, completely bypassing his question as I shift into reverse and peel out of the driveway.

That's an argument that can wait for another day as far as I'm concerned. Besides, I've got my priorities in the right order, and putting Satan's number one slut in her place is top of the fucking list.

"YOU ALRIGHT OVER THERE OR did you lie to me and she actually turned you into a tweaker too?" I ask Red curiously as she rests her head against the passenger's side window. I haven't known the little crazy redhead that long, and it's not like I pay that much attention to her, but I'm pretty confident that she's normally a hell of a lot more energetic than this.

"I'll be fine," she mutters.

"If you say so."

Pulling a cigarette from the pack in the visor, I light one up. I really don't care if she's doing fine or not, but I refuse to have another road trip with a junkie. The first time was bad enough, even when I found out that they had been fucking with me and he wasn't smacked up on the drive. Granted, it just showed me even more that Trixie can get anyone and everyone to do whatever the fuck she wants.

I'm too tired of playing her goddamn games, though. I'm not interested in our constant dick measuring contests even though we haven't had the opportunity in twenty damn years.

I think the only way to show this precious little cunt that she'll only ever be second best is to take away her following.

A fish rots from the head down, after all, but this bitch needs her pond drained to understand that she's nothing special. And if this new and improved Trixie is anything like the old one, once her light worshipping assholes run off and leave her alone, she'll fold because there won't be anyone around to worship her anymore.

Then the kid will see her for what she is, and that's just another win in my book. That cocky brat may think he's won something, but Trixie isn't a goddamn trophy. She's a pathetic addict, and once he sees the truth he'll realize he's just as pathetic as she is.

Crazy girl lets out a quiet groan from the passenger seat and I reach over to turn down the Blondie CD I grabbed from my workshop. She really does look like shit, and that brings up a damn good question.

"Hey, how'd you get back to my place, anyway?" I ask Red. Not that I particularly care, but curiosity has always been a sin of mine.

"Hitchhiked," she answers softly, and I shrug.

"Take a load off. We'll be back in the desert in no time. Then maybe me and you can have a little fun, eh?" I reach over and giving her leg a squeeze.

She grunts and I smirk.

Sometimes, two devils are better than one. Especially when I know that this little red monster is desperate to show me what she's made of.

EIGHT

Freedom from Darkness

AFTYN

The Daughter seems saddened by it, but I'm glad Daphne left. She was nothing but bad memories. The last piece of a rotten history that I don't have to be tethered to anymore.

Of all the things The Daughter has given me *that* is the most precious.

Freedom.

Not just in this new way of life, but freedom from everything in my past that I never realized was so heavy. My mother, my mistakes, my douchebag of a sperm donor, and all of that endless rage that used to drive me forward every damn day.

Sun Wolf said it best when he described how the pain in our histories acts like stones weighing us down in the darkness. In the empty black of our internal pain, we can't even see how those memories, those actions, those *people* have weighed us down.

But The Daughter brings Light to all who seek it out. She shines her Light into us, revealing all of the chains tethering us to our damaged past—and then she sets us free.

She set *me* free.

Walking down the central path of the community, I can feel her Light even though she's in the main hall communing with some of the Children of Light and the higher ranked Light Weavers. I reach over to run my fingers under Willa's hair tie and a smile spreads across my dry lips. The warmth of the sun on my back, combined with the elastic stretch of the band, brings me a greater peace than I ever thought possible.

If Willa were here, she'd appreciate this.

All Wills ever wanted was to make me happy. Sure, we didn't always get along, but that was part of who we were. We challenged each other, pushed each other toward greatness.

Most of all, we protected each other.

She helped me kill my whore of a mother so that I could be free—which is just one more way that Willa and The Daughter are similar. Blonde hair and golden hearts. Freeing the wounded people they find along the way.

Hell, that's what Willa was trying to do with Dexter too, just trying to help him… but he was using her. Abusing her golden heart, and so I'd done what I had to do. It had been my turn to protect her, and that—

Stop it, Aftyn.

Dwelling on the past only drags us further away from the light, and I refuse to ever go back to the person I was before I found this Holy Ground and The Daughter.

Taking a deep breath, I turn my face up to the sky and turn until I can feel the full heat of the sun.

This warmth is Willa.

She's part of the Light now, as we all will be one day, and I can only hope she sees the peace our insane journey eventually brought me to.

I'd been an idiot to think answers or peace or anything good could lie with Lakyn Meyer, but in some roundabout way when I took that first step toward finding him… I *was* on the right path.

I just didn't know the final destination.

"Aftyn." Her soft, sweet voice has me opening my eyes, temporarily blinded by the glorious light of the sun before I turn to look at The Daughter. Although, she's just as blinding. Those golden rays arc around her beautiful blonde hair, catching the fierce shine of the sun and amplifying it. She is Light incarnate, and for the millionth time I find myself wanting to thank her for accepting me—for setting me free.

"Daughter," I eventually reply, but my voice cracks because my throat is too dry. That's why I wandered out here in the first place. I was thirsty, but then I got distracted by thoughts of my past, which shouldn't even happen because they don't matter anymore.

I'm free now, just like all the Children of the Light.

"You look thoughtful this afternoon." The Daughter steps closer to me, her warm, soft hand slipping into mine to squeeze gently. "Are you still thinking of Lakyn?"

"No," I reply a little too sharply and immediately try to soften my tone. "I was thinking about Willa, and how she's in the Light now."

That serene smile slides over her face as she turns it toward the sun, eyes closed as her crown makes her glow. "Yes, she's there. Waiting for the time when we will join her in the Light."

"Which won't be for a long time," I add. Lifting her hand, I place a kiss on her knuckles and then pull her closer, but just as I lean down to kiss her lips... she laughs and turns away. A rush of heat hits my face and I want to yank her back, but then she strokes my cheek, and those blue eyes freeze me in place.

"Oh, Aftyn." She shakes her head, that beautiful smile keeping me transfixed. "I still can't believe Lakyn had a son, and that you found your way to me." Her voice has that dreamy quality, and I know Luminescence or Raindrop likely gave her more of the ambrosia. It irks me because she never quite sees me when she's had it. The sex is fucking amazing after a cup of the stuff, but whenever she's drank it, and I haven't, things are a lot less fun.

"I thought you said you wouldn't bring him up anymore," I remind her, because I'm sure she doesn't actually remember that conversation right now. When her smile doesn't even flicker, I push down the anger and try and focus on the peace I felt just a moment ago, but it's fucking hard. Huffing, I release her hand to shove my hair back from my forehead, but she just winds her arm through mine and turns us back toward the home we share.

"Did I say that?" she asks absently, and I sigh. It's not her fault she's like this. The Daughter just exists in a different way than the rest of us, and I have to remind myself of that sometimes. But I love her, so it's not hard to forgive her, and since forgiveness is just another form of freedom I choose to take that path.

"Yes, Daughter, you did," I answer. My tongue is so dry it sticks to the roof of my mouth as I speak, and I clear my throat. "But I was on my way to get something to drink when you found me. I need to—"

"Sun Wolf has lunch waiting for us."

"Just us?" I ask, looking down at her so I can try and figure out if she's trying to invite Sun Wolf into our bed again. I already told her no on that. She's mine. She was always meant to be mine just like I was meant to end up here. Lakyn was just the dark conduit that brought me to The Daughter.

"Yes, my dear Aftyn. Just us." With those words I feel that heady lightness return, and I know this is the Light working through her again. Whenever we're apart for too long, I can feel the darkness creeping back in, threatening to drag me down again... but she always saves me. She always sets me free again, pushes the empty black away until there is only love and Light.

I can't pretend to be happy when I see Sun Wolf and Luminescence in our house, but the sight of the ceramic pitcher is enough to bring a polite smile to my face.

"Daughter, we've prepared a private meal as you requested," Sun Wolf says, and I feel like I could levitate off the floor. I know how important it is for everyone here to see her, to spend time with her, and that's why I try to give her space when she needs it, but today she *chose* me. Over all of them.

Over Sun Wolf.

Take that, fucker.

My smile is definitely more of a smirk right now, but both of them are too focused on The Daughter to notice.

"Aftyn is thirsty," she says, waving a hand gracefully at the pitcher. "Luminescence, will you pour him a cup?"

"Of course, Daughter."

"Thanks," I say as she hands it over, and even though the scent of the ambrosia hits my nose to warn me it's not water, I still chug the whole damn wooden goblet down. That warm hum kicks off in my stomach a few seconds later, and all I feel is relief that at least she won't be the only one swooning in the Light in a few minutes.

"More?" Luminescence offers, and I wordlessly offer the goblet as I watch Sun Wolf and The Daughter whispering together while he removes her crown.

Jealousy is just another kind of darkness that keeps us away from the Light, but I can't deny feeling it. Just like I can't deny the urge to shove him away from her, but it fades when she smiles at me and I can see that lustful glint in her eye.

Sun Wolf may have her ear, but I'll have her in our bed as soon as these two leave.

"So, we're having lunch in here today?" I ask, gently reminding The Daughter that it's supposed to be a *private* lunch, but it's Sun Wolf who takes the hint.

"Yes. The Daughter has had a busy morning and has requested to spend time with the One True Soul Lover of Light. Please call on us if you need anything." Bowing his head slightly toward The Daughter, he holds out his hand for Luminescence and they leave together, shutting us into the small home we share.

The Daughter steps closer to me and this time when I lean down to kiss her, she doesn't turn away. Her lips are perfect, sweet, and warm, and even though a part of my brain is aware that the rush of tingles over my skin is likely due to the ambrosia, I really don't give a fuck. Every second with her is vibrant and more fulfilling than any night with any whore I've ever bent over the end of a bed.

"You look so much like him," she whispers against my lips, and it's only the rolling heat of the ambrosia that keeps the darkness of my anger at bay.

"Don't talk about him."

"Why, Aftyn?" she asks, tilting her gaze up at me as she trails her fingers over my ribs. "You are a part of him. The best parts of him, from what I can see."

"Right," I scoff.

"You are," The Daughter insists as she reaches up to cup the side of my face. "Just as handsome. Driven. Dedicated. Yet you are capable of holding the Light inside you in a way I fear he's lost."

"Can we just—"

She laughs and I can feel my teeth grinding as I bite down on the suggestion to get in bed.

"What are you laughing at?"

"You," she answers in that soft, dreamy voice and I jerk back from her touch, but she shakes her head slightly. "Not like that, Aftyn. I'm not laughing at *you*, but the idea of you. It seems impossible for you to exist, and yet… here you are. A blessing of the Light out of the bleakest darkness. A piece of hope from the higher planes, meant to bring the Children of the Light a future. Through us."

Us. It always makes me feel better when she says that.

"I love you, Daughter," I whisper, kissing her again as I shift her back toward the bedroom, and she moves with me like we're dancing. Every step she takes is with perfect grace, fluid and magical, and when she laughs again it doesn't even bother me. Instead, it reminds me of the tinkling of wind chimes near the dining area.

In moments we're naked and as I slide my fingers through her wetness, plunging two deep inside, I'm in awe of the way she arches her back and moans softly. I love how freely she reacts. Not shy, not reserved. She moans, grinds against my hand, soaking my fingers as I add a third and lean down to flick my tongue over her clit. Her hand fists my hair, holding me where she wants me for the moment, and I soak in the taste of her, the scent of her.

Mine.

That word rolls like thunder inside me. It's a dark thought, full of possessiveness and vengeance, but I'm okay with it. The Daughter, *Trixie*, is the one thing my bastard of a sperm donor ever wanted and she's mine. She's spreading her legs for me, not him, and all I can hope is that somehow he knows it's happening.

"Come here," she commands, and I shift over her, kissing her so she can taste herself on my tongue, and the hunger in her response has me lining up and thrusting inside her without waiting.

"Is this what you needed, Daughter?" I ask, slamming deep just the way she likes, and I know she does. Those sweet moans are all for me, all mine, and Lakyn fucking Meyer will never get to fuck her like this.

"Yes," she gasps, nails digging into my back as I grab her knee and push it toward her shoulder to get even deeper. "Fill me with your Light, Aftyn. Help me bring about the future for the Children of the Light."

Future. Children.

The words make it through the lust and ambrosia-fueled haze in my head, and I realize what she's asking for… she wants me to knock her up. Just the idea of putting a baby inside her has my balls tingling. It's all the proof anyone would need of my true purpose here, my *right* to stand at The Daughter's side. Lakyn never even got to fuck her when she was Trixie, and now she's everything he wanted to be and I'm going to be the father of her child.

Vengeance really shouldn't be this sweet.

"Say it again," I urge, holding off the need to come even as her cunt grips my cock, begging me to do it.

"Fill me, Aftyn," she pants, moaning in her perfect, soft voice. "Spill your Light inside me so that we can create a future together."

"Our future."

"Yes! Our future!" The Daughter shouts and her pussy clamps down on me like a vise, and it's impossible to resist. I come and the sudden rush of ecstasy is as blinding as the sun was outside. A perfect light that I know I'm putting inside her so that we can start a new path together.

A better path. A brighter one.

Free of all the darkness.

As the world starts to come back into shimmery focus, I take my place beside The Daughter and smile when I feel her pull my hand onto her lower belly. We're both slick with sweat, out of breath from the rush of orgasm, but I lift my head just so I can look at the expanse of skin under my fingers.

Right there could be the beginning of a new life. A part of me and The Daughter growing inside her, cementing our connection in blood. Something that Lakyn Meyer will never have because she would never give it to him. But she chose me, and I feel a chuckle rumbling up in my chest as I stare at her belly because... how funny would it be if we have a daughter?

NINE

Halos & Hatred

DAPHNE

My forehead is pressed against the window of the car. For the second time in the past half an hour, I've wiped my mouth with the back of my hand.

I can't stop salivating and yet, somehow, I still feel so goddamn thirsty.

Lakyn hasn't said much since we left. He put in a CD and has spent most of his time ignoring me.

In a different world—one where everything didn't look so goddamn hazy—I'd be bothered by it. But I welcome it now; I just hope it won't last for too long.

Be the perfect girl and he'll love you forever.

I repeat the mantra to myself over and over. Buried deep inside of me somewhere is still that young child that wants so desperately to be loved and accepted for exactly who she is. No mask, no fake smiles, no polite civil bullshit. Just me.

Lakyn has shown me a sliver of that already and even though it hurt when he left me behind, he chose me to come with him so I want nothing more than to rip open the wound and watch it fester with our love.

Our love.

Not Ichabod's.

Not Aftyn's.

Not that Trixie's either.

Ours.

That's the only thing that's making me fight this sick feeling inside. I know that Ichabod said it's my leg, but I wouldn't be surprised if that Trixie lady had one of her hippies drug me while I was asleep because I wouldn't drink their crazy cactus shit willingly.

They're all so fucking weird there. I hated being abandoned there, and as time went on, and I got even sicker, all I wanted was to be near the one man that would make me feel better.

And now we're together again.

"You okay, Red?" His voice sounds a little thicker than normal which prompts me to steal a glance in his direction.

I sit up almost instantly, which in retrospect isn't the best idea because I almost end up vomiting all over his console when the world spins around me.

But…

"Lakyn," I murmur in awe of what he looks like now.

He lets out a heavy sigh and I reach forward to slip my fingers through the air. I can see the gentle evil that lulls inside of him, waiting until he needs it, and it caresses my skin as I slip my fingers through his breath. Then I sit back and raise my hand in front of my eyes feeling a thousand times better than I did before.

"Lakyn…" I say again, shoving my hand in front of his mouth. I need more of the gentle evil—more than the weirdos in the desert need their cactus water.

She would be so jealous if she could see what healing really looks like, I tell myself as I squint from the pain of him bouncing over a bump in the road.

In the next moment, he takes my wrist between his thumb and forefinger and eases my hand back into my lap.

"Wait," I object as I put the tips of my fingers in front of his mouth again. "I need this."

"What the fuck, Red?" When Lakyn gives me an incredulous look, the beautiful, light-golden halo that's been slowly forming around him shimmers slightly.

"Don't make me leave you on the side of the road," he snarls at me. Even through his mock anger, I can see the golden light around him starting to gain power, shining a little brighter… filling me with more hope.

"Please," I beg him, tears starting to sting my eyes as his power fades from my skin. "Breathe on my fingers again."

He eyes me for a moment before he pushes my hand away from his face and that devilish half-grin takes over his face.

It's now that I realize what's been happening this entire time.

This was never a trip to reunite with the woman in the desert—it's been a mission to reclaim his throne.

The *real* god of the desert is sitting right beside me, and now I can see him for what he really is. A dark god of pure truth. No masks, no pretending. Lakyn is exactly who he wants to be at all times, and he never gives a shit about anyone's expectations.

No, the world bends to *his* will.

It exists only to feed his dark cravings, to entertain him, and I feel like every fucked-up moment in my life has led me to this place at this time just so I could be a witness to his ascension to his rightful place.

A dark, beautiful god.

A force of nature.

The waves of golden light pulsing off him are tinged with a core of black that speaks to whatever version of a soul I possess. It's overwhelming to be this close to him, close enough to touch if I dared—but I don't.

He's too perfect to touch.

Being next to him is all I need, and now that the waves of dark light are filling the car, I can feel the energy healing me. The throbbing pain in my thigh starts to recede, the swishy feeling in my head fading. Then he looks at me and instead of blue eyes, I see nothing but black. No whites, just raw darkness. Honest and powerful, and it steals my breath away.

"Hail Lakyn," I whisper softly before I can't take the absolute brilliance of him anymore. Then I close my eyes and slump over in my seat.

A SHARP JOLT bounces my head against the window and I sit up with a grunt.

I don't know how long I've been asleep, and I really don't care as long as Lakyn hasn't dumped me somewhere and moved on without me.

I put my hands on the console to steady myself, taking comfort that I'm still in his car. At least, that's my hope because with him anything is possible. He has the power to accomplish anything.

"Lakyn?" I mumble.

"Yep, still here. Still driving, still bored out of my fucking mind. Take a good nap, Red?" he asks in a disinterested tone.

"Sorry," I say quietly as another wave of nausea crashes over me followed quickly by a chill that has my teeth chattering.

"Hey, sleep is a good thing. I like it myself and hope to crash sometime soon, so don't worry about it," he replies with a chuckle.

I nod as I push myself off the door hard enough that I can finally rest back against the seat. My head rolls in Lakyn's direction and I smile tiredly when I see the halo is still there.

"You're so beautiful," I murmur.

He laughs. "Nothing I didn't already know, Red."

My smile widens a little as I reach toward his lips again—if I can just get another breath of the gentle evil he harbors inside of him, it'll make me feel even better.

"Stop doing that," he snaps as he slaps my hand away. "I get that you want to touch me, but this is starting to get a little creepy."

"You don't understand…" I sigh as I shake my head.

"Sure I do, but that's going to have to wait, and not a word of it to Ichabod. Not that he would believe you, but I don't want to deal with anymore of his bitching. Takes the fun out of the house for a day or two."

Lakyn isn't glowing as brightly as he was before, but I can still see the aura around him. A golden shimmer with a dark heart that seems to fit him perfectly. *This* is what Ichabod, and Aftyn, and that Beatrix bitch have never seen in Lakyn. They don't see him like I do, they don't understand how perfect he is, which makes me wonder why he'd ever keep someone like Ichabod around him that doesn't see him for who he is.

"Do… do you love him?"

I don't know why I asked that or where it came from, but that young, lost girl inside of me needs to know more than I thought she did. I need to know if I have a chance here, or if this dark god plans to leave me in the desert again. I don't think I'll survive it if he does.

"Come again?" he asks in disbelief as he lowers the radio.

"Ichabod. Do you love him?" I press quietly.

"What the fuck is up with everyone lately? First some kid that barely looks like me shows up on my doorstep telling me I shot a load into his mother. Then the ole ball and chain gets pissy because I didn't bring him Satan's Superstar. You're clearly way further out of your goddamn mind than I thought"—he says as his finger spins a circle next to his temple—"and I'm in a goddamn car going to Beatrix. *Again*, I might add, which if you must know already has me in a pretty piss poor mood. So, one more time, and I want you to think long and hard before you decide to answer me, okay? What the fuck did you just ask me?"

He ends his tirade in a hiss, and I smile when I see what I was after starting to linger in the air again.

"God of the Desert," I whisper as my fingers reach out toward his breath.

"What?" he asks in confusion.

"Nothing," I answer as I sit up as best as I can and turn in my seat to face him.

Because of his anger, the halo looks fractured, and I worry that it will never be whole again. But that will only make us even more alike since I haven't felt like a whole person in a long time. Maybe ever.

Have I ever been real?

"Listen," he says as he clears his throat and reaches up in the visor for his pack of cigarettes. "When we get back to the Garbage Land of Bullshit, I may need you to take out Trixie. Think you can do that?"

I nod and wrap my arms around myself. I may not be on my A-game right now, but I'll do whatever he needs me to do—especially since that will eliminate someone else that he cares for.

He nods as he places a cigarette between his teeth, then lights it. When he inhales, I anticipate the exhalation of his healing power, but this time it's not shimmering or golden.

It's black and cancerous, and that's how I know that the evil inside of him isn't gentle at all—it's rawer than that. He's like a tiger, absolutely beautiful to look at, but incredibly dangerous. Lethal. Unforgiving.

It makes me wonder, though.

If the beautiful exterior is the Lakyn Meyer that he presents to the world, what does the one underneath that look like?

I'll find out once and for all when we get back to the desert. I'll feed his hatred and disdain for being second best to Trixie again and I'll finally get to see the real Lakyn in all of his glory.

Then he'll see that we're not so different after all.

TEN

Hell is Here

ICHABOD

I can't sit still.

It's not that I haven't tried, but there's only so much shitty television I can watch while this cancerous hope eats away at my insides.

I shouldn't believe him. It's so damn stupid to keep believing him, but I know that Lakyn feels for Bea in his own way. They were connected long before I met him, and they'll probably be connected long after he finally gets bored of me and I end up in that tub as an oozing, stinking puddle of something that used to be a person.

Not like I feel like a person anymore.

But… I always did when Bea looked at me. There was something about the way her eyes really *saw* me, the way her entire face lit up when she smiled at me that made me feel like I was worth something. Like it fucking mattered that my heart kept beating from one second to the next.

It's just been so goddamn long since I felt that way and thinking about it makes the lack of it hurt all the more. It makes the waiting around even more impossible, and it's why I keep checking out the front curtains even though there isn't a chance in hell they could be back yet.

"You better keep this promise, Lakyn," I mutter to myself in the dead silence of the house.

Heh.

Dead silence.

The phrase brings a bitter, hushed laugh out of me and I turn around to look at the door to Lakyn's little workshop of horrors.

When I was on the streets, I thought that was hell. I thought the drugs, and the humiliation, and the filth were how the demons chose to torment me... and then Bea had been my angel. No matter what choices she made, no matter what snide comments Lakyn has made about her, she reached into hell to give me comfort. To show me kindness.

Love.

I just want to feel it one more time now that I've really found hell—because Lakyn is absolutely the devil and this house is his throne. The central point from which he causes so much pain. Kills, tortures, destroys, all while laughing or singing in that way that makes him impossible to look away from despite how terrible it all is. He's as beautiful as an angel, but filled by so much darkness, and that's why I need Bea back.

Whenever I was drowning in darkness, she was always able to pull me out for a little while. A hug, a smile, some warm food, and I would get a sip of fresh air, a hint of light, and then I'd be alright for a bit.

I know that if I can just see her again, have her look at me and *see* me the way she used to… I'll be okay. I'll be able to survive however many days I have left here in hell.

Sitting down in Lakyn's chair, I can't help the fidgeting, so I light a cigarette and take a short puff of it before setting it in the ashtray. The way the smoke curls upward is hypnotic, and I wish I could say it's relaxing… but it isn't.

Nothing about me is relaxed right now.

I'm drawn tight, like a string about to snap from being tuned too far, which I'm sure would entertain Lakyn if he were here. He always likes to wind me up, to see if I'll grow a spine instead of suffering in silence and emptiness.

Which is why the smell of the goddamn cigarette smoke shouldn't be comforting, and I hate myself because it is.

Somehow, being alone in hell, without the devil, is worse than anything else, and the scent of the smoke is enough to make me just a little less shaky.

I don't take my eyes off the door though, and I know that in another minute I'll be checking out the window again, because hope is the one thing that suffering in hell hasn't been able to completely destroy inside me yet.

I still have hope that I'll get one last glimpse of the sun, one last breath of fresh air, before there's only darkness left.

And I'll get it. I have to.

As soon as Lakyn keeps his promise and brings Bea back to me.

ELEVEN

Daddy Issues

AFTYN

We're both slick with sweat, and I'm too hot right now, but I can't take my hand off The Daughter's belly.

She could be pregnant right now.

I could be a dad.

The idea brings a smile to my lips, and I press my fingers into her skin just a little bit as I make a silent promise to the tiny life that I hope is forming.

I don't care if you're a boy or a girl, but I swear I'll be a good dad to you. I'll be all the things for you I wish my mother had been, and I'll never hurt you. I'll never be ashamed of you. I'll make sure you know you're loved. Every damn day. I promise.

The Daughter stretches, and the roll of her hips breaks my contact with her belly, but it's fine. It knows how I feel, and I'll be here to watch her belly grow, and I'll be there when they're born. When she turns to look at me, my throat feels suddenly dry, but her smile gives me courage.

"Do… do you think it worked?" I whisper, and my voice sounds funny in my ears, but I keep looking at the smooth expanse of her stomach, imagining it swelling and I have to believe it's true.

She just smiles at me in that infinite way and brushes her hand over my cheek, drawing my gaze back to hers.

"Do you?" I repeat.

"Perhaps. Only the Light will show us the truth of it, dear Aftyn," she answers softly.

"I think it did." I nod, because in this moment I can feel the Light within me, speaking to me, speaking *through* me. "I feel a kind of connection."

"To me?" The Daughter asks, and I lean down to kiss her. Her lips are warm, still sweet from all of the ambrosia we drank, and the way my skin tingles from her touch is just more recognition of her power. *Our* power now, because we're united in one of the most important ways two people can be.

A new life.

"Aftyn?" she says my name on a laugh and the light, tinkling sound of it makes me laugh too.

"I've felt connected to you from the first moment I saw you." I run my hand down her side and rest it on her belly again. "Now, it's just… deeper."

"I knew you were the right choice," she whispers, and I lean down to kiss her again when I hear voices outside and the distant sound of an engine just before someone bangs on the door.

"Daughter, there is someone coming up the drive."

Fucking Sun Wolf. Of course.

"Ignore him," I whisper.

She looks at me and shakes her head, brushing her thumb over my lips before she sits up. "We must welcome them, whoever the lost souls may be. It's our duty to the Light, our calling."

Our duty. Our calling.

It's all I've wanted since I first saw her. To be a part of her, to be connected to her, to be an *us*.

The only other person I've ever felt that with is Willa. *Was* Willa. But I have it again with The Daughter, and I have to believe that Wills had a hand in this. She's in the Light now, which means she can see the way the world is designed, can see my destiny, and she's helped me find it.

Wills helped me find The Daughter... and my future.

"You're right. It's our duty." My answer brings a bright smile to her face, like the Light is radiating from her in waves, and in another minute we're both dressed and opening the door to see Sun Wolf and Luminescence waiting for us.

"Little Star has returned to us," Luminescence says with the absolute joy that everyone here feels.

"We should welcome her back," The Daughter replies, but when she starts to walk forward Sun Wolf stops her.

"Wait, Daughter. You should wear the Light." He slips past her into our home and returns with the golden crown, tucking it into her hair and pinning it in place so that everyone will see the rays of Light around her head.

"Thank you, Sun Wolf," she says, smiling at him, but it's not the same way she smiles at me. It means more when it's directed at me, and soon he'll see just how different he and I are. All of his longing looks at her will be just that. Longing.

I offer my arm and she takes it, and Sun Wolf and Luminescence fall into step behind us as we head toward the steadily rising cloud of dust that the vehicle stirred up. The sky looks like it's on fire, vibrant oranges and reds signaling the setting sun, and all of the colors seem to reflect in the golden spikes around her head. It makes The Daughter look like some mirage from the desert, like something from a fairy tale… and I'm at her side.

Where I belong.

Many of the Children of the Light are gathering in the main walk of the community, and as we pass they all smile. It's pure adoration in their eyes. For The Daughter, and now for me too. For us.

It fills me with a sense of purpose, of *meaning* that I've never had in my life, and for a second I feel like I'm walking on air. I know that part of the light, bubbly feeling is all the ambrosia we drank, but part of it is real too, and it feels like it could last forever.

Then I see him.

The air behind him is hazy with dust, and the setting sun seems to be playing tricks on my eyes because the dust itself seems stained red with blood. Like a fine mist of it is just hovering behind him, and *her*.

I should be beyond the hate I feel for both of them, but there it is. Simmering underneath all of the goodness that The Daughter has brought out in me, begging me to make the haze of blood real.

"I knew he'd return to us." The Daughter unwinds her arm from mine and walks toward them like she can't see the hatchet resting on his shoulder, glinting in the light.

"He can't be here," I whisper to her as soon as I catch up to her side, but when I try to grab her elbow, she pulls away to spread her arms wide in welcome to the bastard that doesn't belong here.

Lakyn fucking Meyer doesn't deserve to be here.

I won't let him take this from me.

This is my destiny. The destiny that Wills brought me. I was meant to be at The Daughter's side, and it's *our* calling to lead the others into the Light.

And he doesn't belong in the Light.

He belongs six feet under, bled out, and even though I know that's a dark thought I can't keep it at bay because of the fucking smirk on his face as he blows out a cloud of smoke and takes a single step toward us before we all stop moving.

Lakyn adjusts the hatchet on his shoulder and sucks on his teeth, tilting his head from side to side as he glances at me before settling his gaze on the one he calls Trixie. A low chuckle rolls out of him as he spreads one arm out in a mockery of The Daughter's welcome, and that damn grin slides over his lips.

"Miss me?"

TWELVE

Gods in the Desert pt. 1

LAKYN

It's clear to me that Trixie is still smacked up on her fucking cactus water, and it's even more clear to me that these two are coming down from the high of a fresh fuck.

So Red wasn't lying to me after all.

"I'm so happy that you've decided to return—"

"Shut the fuck up," I snarl at Trixie. Because while I have a few words of my own for her, I'm waiting for the right moment to let that happen.

Running a blood-soaked hand back through my hair, I take a deep breath and let it out as the grin returns to my lips. It's been such a long time since I've been able to really let go and get down and dirty, but this… this is special. I almost don't feel like doing what I know has to be done.

Almost.

"So…" I begin as my eyes turn toward the kid. The way he's standing, inched in front of Trixie, and trying to block me from seeing her, makes this all the sweeter. "You know, I gotta ask, what made you crawl under this used up bitch? Was it mommy issues or daddy ones?"

The kid goes rigid, squaring his jaw and clenching his fists. I decide to remind him that he's literally one wrong move away from joining his whore of a mother by shifting the hatchet from one shoulder to the other. His eyes follow my lead, watching the freshly sharpened blade glinting in the sunlight. Even after a nice dip into some Sun Fuckers' necks and faces, it still shines. I think the blood stains really make it glisten more than when it's dry.

Kind of how I feel about this entire situation in front of me right now. It would look a hell of a lot better covered in blood.

"You don't belong here," Aftyn tells me in a low, trembling voice and I feign fear as I raise a hand, level it with his eyes and shake it. I figure it's the nice thing to do since he's trying so goddamn hard to make something of himself right now.

Red groans next to me and I arch an eyebrow down at her as she sways on her feet. It's so damn easy to forget she's around, but as long as we're here…

"Hey, Sun Fucker," I call out to the pussy behind Trixie. "Be a dear and get Red something to make her feel better. None of that hippie drug water or else." I punctuate my point by running a thumb across my neck. They may not understand much of anything on the bullshit they've been sipping, but death is a universal language—regardless of what planet they seem to be hippie worshipping on.

Big Tits looks at Trixie, presumably waiting for her to say it's okay to help Red, and unfortunately for her, I'm not in the mood for this.

"Suit yourself," I say with a shrug.

Gripping the hatchet firmly in my hand, I move quickly, pushing Trixie and the kid aside, and swing it as hard as I can. Big Tits' eyes go wide—in fear, pain, shock—who the fuck knows or cares.

People are screaming, running, but I don't really care much about the sun fucks. As Big Tits tips over and hits the ground, I grin and tilt my head. This really is no one's fault but her own. What about the bloodstains on me didn't explain that I mean business right now is beyond me.

And now it's beyond her too.

I crouch down over her and run a hand back through her hair. "Tell the other Sun Fuckers that I'll be sending more along soon."

She sputters, sending a small pool of blood bursting out of her mouth like a geyser and I laugh. Looks like I hit her in the right place, and she'll be dead soon enough.

Considering I'm not exactly known for being merciful, I think it'll be best if she just chokes to death on her own blood. Honestly, she's pretty lucky.

Standing back up, I reach for the handle and grunt as I extract it from her throat and another spurt colors the dirt under her.

"Nice!" I exclaim in appreciation. "I haven't seen a wound like that in a while!"

Clearing my throat, I roll my shoulders as I wipe the hatchet off on my jeans then smile at the final four.

The kid looks like he's about to be sick.

Sun Fucker the Sequel is wailing on his knees like a fucking banshee.

Red is looking at me through whatever's making her sick with those goddamn stars in her eyes again.

And Trixie…

Well, Trixie isn't looking at me at all.

She's standing with her back to me, a hand on the kid's arm, the other on the wailer's shoulder, and her face tilted up toward the sky.

"If you're trying to do some kind of mumbo jumbo bullshit on me, Trixie, remember—

your goat is south, not north," I say as I walk around them to look into her eyes.

But they're closed.

Her entire body is rigid and even now, in the ruins of a massacre, this bitch finds a way to make it all about her and push me down a rung again.

"You... you killed her," the kid manages to croak out.

"I... I... sure did," I mock him before I suck my teeth. The rage takes over again in his eyes and I really wish he'd understand just once that I don't give a fuck about him. What happened to Big Tits could happen to anyone, him included.

"Alright, let's try this again," I say loudly. Red leans her body against mine and I roll my eyes up at the sky. *Heh. Maybe something up there will hear me before it hears the Daughter of Smack and Trash.* Dismissing the thought immediately, I reach the hatchet over and tap the remaining Sun Fucker on the head with it. "Got something that'll help Red or do you want to go to the 'Light' ahead of schedule too?"

He falls forward in a frantic attempt to get to his feet. It's nice to know that at least one person here is taking me seriously enough to do what they're fucking told the first time.

"Ah, ah, ah!" I say holding up a finger toward the kid when he tries to follow the Sun Fucker. "Stay. Daddy has a special surprise for you and if you leave, you'll miss it."

He gives me the evil eye which I find endearing. Maybe if I was in the same galaxy these morons have managed to smack themselves into, I might even feel proud. But as it stands, my feet are on the ground here on Earth and I'm not in the least bit interested in understanding the fucked-up way they think.

I glance down at Red and nudge her. She looks up at me with that faint adoration in her eyes and I grin. "Hang in there, kid. We'll get you fixed up here in no time."

"Seriously?"

I turn my attention back to Aftyn and raise an eyebrow. "Hm?"

"You're actually worried about her? What about *me*? You never once gave me a chance.

You never once gave Willa a chance! You just wrote us both off as soon as you could, and kept her around?"

By the time he's done shouting his diatribe, I find myself becoming bored. I roll my eyes, reach over, drape an arm around Red's shoulders, and shrug.

But I don't say anything to what he's been babbling about because I refuse to let someone else call me a liar.

I already had enough of that bullshit at home. No need to bring it into the wastelands since doing that will only make me lose my mojo.

"Anywaaaaayyy… while we wait for him to hippie his way back and forth, I got a question for you, Trixie," I begin as I start to sway side to side. I'm starting to get tired of her closed eyes bullshit and if she doesn't open them soon, I'll cut the lids off her goddamn skull. "Don't make me say it again, girlie," I growl at her.

She opens her eyes slowly and I turn my face away for a moment. For no other reason than I've finally gotten to the point in my life where

I can't stand looking at her and I'm so over her hierarchy bullshit that I'm liable to snap.

"Lakyn," she says softly as her eyes come into focus.

I click my tongue against the back of my teeth and roll my eyes again. "Ichabod is fucked up over not seeing you again. I promised him that I would bring you back for a little feelings-fuck-circle. Then, when I got home, and you weren't there, know what that made me look like? A liar. Know what he called me? A liar. Now, what's the one thing I never am or have been?"

Aftyn snickers and I give him a withering stare. "Don't you worry, mistake of the century, I'll get to you shortly."

He blanches, his shoulders slump a little, and I smirk. If he hasn't guessed that I give zero fucks about his existence yet, then that's his problem.

"Well, bitch?" I snap at Trixie.

She shakes her head as she lets go of Aftyn's arm and clasps her hands together in front of her. *Here we go with the demi-god delusions.*

"I'm doing my best to recall my past life," she begins slowly. Trixie reaches up and rearranges her pointy crown, then runs her hands through her hair before she chews her lower lip thoughtfully. "And try as I might, I don't recall anyone by that name."

I somehow manage not to let my mouth fall open. I don't know why I thought she would have answered differently this time, but the fact that she's so fucking out of it that she can't remember the man whose life she stole, ruined, then sold off, absolutely boggles my goddamn mind.

"That isn't even remotely close to what I wanted to know," I say after I swallow the rage back down. I let go of Red and give her a gentle shove away from me. I'm barely holding onto the little bit of control I have left, and having my number one fan feeling me up, thinking I don't realize the subtle bullshit she's doing, is going to send me over the edge.

"Daughter!"

I turn to glance over my shoulder, the grin returns, and I'm starting to feel better already.

The Sun Fucker looks so damn scared and frantic that I know he's finally stumbled on the little gift I've left for Trixie. But he's emptyhanded, and that won't do.

"Before you open your mouth," I say to him in an even tone. "Where's the shit for Red?"

He falls to his knees and starts to blubber again, and I shake my head.

"You know, Trixie, when you were on your quest to become Satan's Superstar, you hung with a far better crop of wannabes. All these do is cry and drink druggie water. I guess having a cult isn't as great as you thought it would be, eh? At least there would be non-stop fucking in mine."

"What ails you, Sun Wolf?" she asks, ignoring me completely.

"They're dead," he manages to spit out between his heaving sobs. "I went... t-to the... Cactus... and..."

"*Tsk, tsk.* You ruined the surprise!" I chide him in a cheerful tone.

When he turns his eyes up toward me, they're full of hatred. There's no light left in that washed up hippie body of his, so I do the one thing that I would want someone to do for me if I ever turned into a drugged-out follower.

I pull my arm back and throw the hatchet so fucking hard, that it breaks the sound barrier as it flies toward him. A loud, sickening crack, and Sun Wolf falls back with a *thud*.

"Looks like I've still got it," I say with a laugh. "I haven't tossed that thing in a few years so it's good to know that my aim never fell off." I snap my fingers at Red, who looks up at me, her eyes still a little hazy and she nods. While she's busy trying to yank the hatchet out of ole Wolfy's face, I turn to face Trixie and Aftyn again.

Crossing my arms over my chest, and chuckling at the grunts behind me, I wait for her to answer my initial question.

I can see the tears starting to brim in her doped-up eyes as the kid puts an arm protectively around her.

Red shoves the handle of the hatchet in my hand before she wobbles on her feet again.

"Hey, think you can make it to ground zero on your own?" I ask her. She looks up at me and shrugs. "Tell you what, you go back to where we left the hippies to rot in the sun, drink some of that cactus shit and when we get home, I'll ween you off that shit like I did with Ichabod, okay?"

Red uses the back of her hand to wipe her mouth. "But you hate drugs."

"I mean, if you'd rather die here, then by all means," I continue with a shrug.

But I know Red better than she knows herself, and the prospect of living under my roof is more than enough to make her fight for her own life, which is something I really care nothing about. I just need her alive long enough to bear witness.

I watch her over my shoulder, waiting until she's gone from view, before I turn my attention back to the odd couple.

"Well, I guess this is it, huh?"

Aftyn tenses, his jaw squaring and I can't help but laugh. He gives up his position way too easily and that's why I'd never be able to really give a shit about him.

At least with Ichabod there's *some* mystery to how he's feeling about things.

Or at least there used to be, I think as I scratch the back of my head.

"Remember when you and Ichabod had me tied up in the back of the van, Trixie? How I told you to be fair and give me a chance to defend myself? Remember what you said?"

A tear rolls down her face as the grin starts to grow wider on mine.

I can see the answer on the tip of her tongue. She knows exactly what she said to me and what happened after, but she's so fucking stubborn in wanting to maintain what we're both now recognizing as a façade, that she shakes her head instead of answering.

"'Fuck fair'," I remind her softly.

A sigh escapes me as I crack my neck and think of Ichabod. I know that she cares about him and no amount of smack water will ever erase the memory of their lives together away completely.

And just as I'm starting to think of changing my mind, the kid pulls his shirt over his head and gives Trixie a shove back.

"Go Daughter. Save yourself, save our child. It's the only way to bring life to the Holy Ground of Light again."

"Your… your what?" I ask, my voice trembling slightly. My body starts to follow suit and I'm getting to the point where I won't be able to hold onto this hatchet much longer if I keep shaking like this.

"Surprise, *Dad*," the kid says evenly with a sinister smile on his face. "I'm going to be a father, and you know what? That's something else that I'll have with The Daughter that you never will."

What. The. Fuck.

The world looks different through shades of fury and rage. White, red, and even a little black around the edges.

"Run, piggy," I snarl at Trixie who immediately turns on her heel and hauls ass. The best part of a kill is the chase, and I'm damn good at both. Granted, she gets to live to see another day since I told Ichabod that I'd be back this time with the bitch in tow. The kid however…

"What's the matter? You too macho to run with your bitch?" I ask him as the black edges begin to form a frame around him.

"I'm not afraid of you, Lakyn," he spits back at me.

"First, and may I add, last mistake," I reply with a grin.

Before the kid has a chance to react, I rush him and slam the hatchet against his chest. His eyes go wide as he tries to take a deep breath, so I clip him with the handle and drop him onto his ass. Once he's down, I kick him in the face to make this easier on myself. I really thought he'd put up more of a fight than this when I decided to erase this mistake, but he's too damn drugged-out to be worth my time. Raising the hatchet over my head, I bring it down into his chest, laughing when the blood flies and the sweet *crack* of his ribs greets my ears.

"D... a... d... S... t... o... p."

I roll my eyes as I drop a knee into his chest and smack his shitty hair out of his face. When his eyes close, more than likely swimming in the agony he has to be feeling, I slap the palm of my free hand against his forehead to open them again.

"Hey," I bark at him, watching his eyes come in and out of focus. "Before you wander off into that precious light of yours, there's something I want you to take with you. That Willa girl? I guarantee she never loved you. I *never* would have given you a chance past what you already got, and this…" I reach down and remove the black hair tie from his wrist, slipping it onto mine. "This stays with me."

He makes a desperate grab to get the little bauble he's been holding onto since his bitch friend died, and I get to my feet before his fingers even have a chance to graze it one last time.

With a grunt, I yank the hatchet free to raise it over my head again and bring it down with such fury that I know it'll probably stay where I've managed to bury it.

Right between his bullshit, *daddy please love me*, eyes.

Cracking my neck, I put my hands on my knees in an attempt to catch my breath before I go see where Trixie has gone. Things like this were a lot easier twenty years ago, but to my credit, it's not just these three dipshits I killed; I took out a bunch of the commune on my way up to the love shack.

"I should probably take you with me," I tell Aftyn as I step over him and reach for the handle. "Bringing Trixie back won't be as easy since she's not the carefree little wondercunt I remember her being."

Taking a deep breath, I begin to drag his still twitching body in the direction I saw Trixie run in. I know where I'll find her because she's never been very smart, no matter how much she tried to be.

It takes me a little longer to walk to the love shack, but when I kick the door open, the bang echoes throughout the fucking place and I can hear Trixie gasp. Glancing to my left, I smirk before I turn around, put both hands on the handle, and yank the kid in with one final pull.

"Here's your fucking sacrifice, Trixie," I say as she puts a hand on her stomach and takes a step backwards. "Now, do I have your attention, little girl?"

THIRTEEN

Sacrificial Lambs

BEATRIX

It feels like the air is suddenly too thin and too warm. Lakyn Meyer fills the doorway of my little house and memories are flickering in my head.

Memories that *should* be dead and buried with the woman he wants to speak to so desperately. Deep in the desert ground.

But something about him is bringing them to the surface. The way he's covered in blood with that merciless grin on his face, the hatchet buried in Aftyn's head... all of it seems to tug at a forgotten part of me.

Horrifying and familiar.

Sacrifices. We've done this before.

"Trixie!" he snaps, and my gaze jerks back to his blue eyes, so much like Aftyn's and yet so different. So much colder and more hateful and connected to that woman that doesn't exist. "You have one chance to answer me, bitch, because I—"

"I remember," I whisper, holding up one hand to keep him back while the other clings to the dress covering my belly. The words are a half-truth, because I don't quite remember, but there are flickering images in my mind.

A thin boy with a sweet face.

A van.

The scent of cigarette smoke.

Lakyn's wild grin.

And blood.

By the Light… so much blood.

"You remember now?" Lakyn asks, chuckling under his breath as he leans against the doorframe and pulls out a pack of cigarettes with blood-soaked fingers. "What do you remember, Trixie?"

Trixie. Trixie. Trixie.

That name is like a rope around my ankle, dragging me down into the darkness under the greenhouse. Pulling me further and further away from the Light, and I have to fight it. I have a purpose, a mission.

"Jesus fucking Christ, are you really so high you can't even talk?" Lakyn blows out a cloud of smoke as he shakes his head. "Not worth the goddamn trouble. I just need to put you out of your misery."

"Wait!" I shout, feeling my muscles tremble as he tugs at the handle of the hatchet. The memories are still a jumbled, fuzzy mess, but I know with absolute certainty that he'll kill me if I let him—and then everything will be lost. The Children of the Light are scattered or dead, but I still carry the future inside me.

I just have to make him believe me.

"I remember the van. You, and me, and the boy—"

"Ichabod," he growls, narrowing his eyes at me as he flicks his cigarette, letting the ashes fall onto Aftyn's blood-soaked shirt.

"Yes, yes. Ichabod. We traveled together for a time, but we were trapped in darkness. Darkness and blood and… wait!" I jerk back as Lakyn suddenly moves toward me, finding myself backed against the doorway into the bedroom. "Please, Lakyn, if you'll just let the Light in you'll see."

"I'm not listening to your hippie light bullshit anymore, Trixie. Time to meet your goat, or your fucking sun bitch, or whatever you're sacrificing to these days." With one more yank of the hatchet, he pulls it free of Aftyn's once-beautiful face and I feel my stomach roll. He was my One True Soul Lover of Light, the father of the child that I *know* is growing inside me, and the most important thing is that I protect that Light. Our future.

Our calling.

It's all on my shoulders now, as The Daughter of the Light I have to rebuild from the ashes, and the only way to protect the Light now is to let my darkness out once more. For so long she's wanted to be free again, to roam the Earth as she once did, and with Lakyn's blood-spattered smirk in front of me I know now is the time all my visits below the greenhouse have prepared me for.

I must walk through the darkness once more in order to prevail in the Light.

"You want me to be Trixie again, Lakyn?" I ask, and the way he swings the hatchet up onto his shoulder tells me all I need to know.

He's still in the mood to play with his food, which means I still have time to slit his fucking throat for ruining everything I've built.

"You want me to prove to you that I remember you and Ichabod?" I let out a little laugh as I glance down at the flowy dress I've got on. It's pretty much the opposite of the shit I used to wear, but it served me well here. This place that he hates so much because it's *mine*. "What do you think of *my* cult, Lakyn? You always wanted something like this. A bunch of people bowing to your every whim, hanging on your every word... but you never actually had the balls to do it, did you?"

"Trixie," he says in a voice low with warning, but I scoop up the knife I would use on our ceremonial altar with fruit instead of lives. I flip it through my fingers, remembering how I used to use things like this before the Light. Before I created 'The Daughter.' Before I turned a bunch of mewling hippies in the desert into a fucking army ready to act on my word. *Before* Lakyn showed up and ruined everything.

"Tut, tut, tut… You wanted to talk to Trixie, and now that I've come out to play, you want me to stop talking?"

"I never liked listening to you, Trixie. What the fuck makes you think I want to listen to you now?" he asks before taking a long drag on his cigarette.

"Well, it has been a while. Don't you want to catch up? I mean… what the fuck have you been doing all these years, Lakyn?" Waving a hand at Aftyn's corpse, another laugh bubbles past my lips. "*Other* than apparently leaving one of your playthings alive. When did that happen exactly?"

"Remember Vegas?" he asks, and I'm irritated that he still seems to be enjoying himself. This piece of shit never did understand his place in my life, and all he's ever done is fuck things up for me—just like he did today. This was *my* cult. *My* worshippers. *My* future.

"Vegas?" I tap my bottom lip with the point of the knife as another movie reel of flickering images pass behind my eyes. That big fucker with his Frankenstein tendencies, the drugs, all of the goddamn problems Lakyn caused even back then.

Damn. Was that really twenty years ago?

"Wow, Lakyn. You started slipping up way back then?" Trailing the knife down the front of my dress, I can't help but smile at how fucking predictable Lakyn still is as his eyes follow the path. Always thinking with his dick. No real plan, no concept of artistry or theater. He's always been an overgrown man-child with a hatchet. "Such a disappointment."

"I'm a disappointment?" he asks, then sucks his teeth, giving me that look I've seen a hundred times before. It's what death looks like. Sure, he's older, but even I have to admit he still looks good even while uselessly planning my death.

I'm not worried though.

He never was able to kill me no matter how much he threatened. He always wanted me just a little more than he wanted me dead.

"Well, yeah, Lakyn. Though I guess, really, you're more a disappointment to yourself, right?" Spreading my arms, I smile at him. "As you know, I haven't thought about you in years. You've been thinking about me though, haven't you? About everything you wanted in life, but were never quite able to obtain?"

"Such as?" he hisses, and I pluck at the dress, swaying my hips back and forth.

"Aww, Lakyn. You're smarter than that." Reaching up, I pull the golden crown free and look at the beautiful, shiny points. "This is just one thing you wanted. To be worshipped, like I have."

I wave my arm toward the doorway, where I know so many of my followers are dead at his hands.

"To have acolytes, ready and willing to act upon your word. Like Manson did... like I did... until your latest temper tantrum anyway."

"Because you drugged them," Lakyn interjects and I shrug, setting the crown down in its place.

"Does it really matter *how*, Lakyn?"

"Yes!" he shouts, shifting his grip on the hatchet to point it at me. "There's two fucking things I hate. Blondes, and druggies, and you've managed to become both of those things, Trixie. Once upon a time you entertained me *just* enough to earn the right to breathe, but after this shit? No fucking way."

Waggling the knife back and forth, I flash the smile that used to either excite Lakyn or infuriate him depending on his mood. "Tsk, tsk, tsk… we both know you're not going to kill me, Lakyn."

"Why's that?"

Moving closer, I nudge the hatchet off his shoulder slowly and lean in until my lips are just a breath from his. "Because you've always wanted me."

"Hmm…" Lakyn drops his cigarette onto Aftyn beside us before gently cupping my cheek. For a moment he almost reminds me of

Aftyn. Gentle, kind, but when his hand glides down to my throat and tightens, I recognize the glint of violence in his eyes.

"S-stop," I choke out, but he just tightens his grip on my throat until I can't squeak out another sound. Cold fear fills my stomach, right next to the life I know Aftyn and I created. The last bit of Light in this rapidly darkening place.

"You spout a lot of bullshit, Trix, but you make a good point. I told you I'd fuck you one day, and like I said before… I always keep my promises." Lakyn's grin is manic, wild, and I suddenly remember everything. I remember every time I saw him look just like this as he picked up a blonde at a bar to take home to his twisted party room. I remember their screams, the hatchet I used that was a twin to the one in his other hand. The blood. So much fucking blood… and I loved it. I loved every damn minute of it while I traded it for power and strength, and Lucifer provided all of it. Everything I asked for I got. *Here*.

And now Lakyn wants to take it for himself.

He grins as he leans in to lick my cheek, his lips right against my ear. "Your cunt is probably a rancid hole by now, but I doubt this idiot was fucking that pert ass of yours, was he?"

I shake my head and manage to steal a thin breath, but he has an iron grip on my throat and soon my head is swimming again. I have to fight. It's the only chance I have, but when I try to jab the knife into his side, he knocks my arm away with the hatchet and a searing pain tells me the sharp edge just cut me. A thin squeak that was meant to be a shout is all I can get out as he shoves me backward until my legs hit the bed and then I can breathe.

Air burns its way into my lungs with a rough gasp, and I cough on the next agonizing inhale while he laughs.

Fuck. I remember that laugh… and I remember what happens next.

"Lakyn!" I manage to croak out his name as I turn to crawl off the bed, to run, but then he's on top of me.

"That's it, Trixie. Struggle for me, put up a fight," he says, shoving my blood-spattered dress up over my hips.

"Get off me!" I shout into the sheets that still smell like Aftyn, like both of us, and even though I never loved him the way he loved me, I still miss him in this moment. Just a little while ago everything was so much simpler, so much easier.

"This is pathetic. You used to be a lot faster when you were Satan's number one bitch." Lakyn grabs a fistful of my hair to crane my neck back painfully far. "But you just had to join this druggie commune so you could be head bitch of the light side instead. *That* is where you fucked up, Beatrix. Drugs are where you always fuck up."

Drugs.

Ichabod.

"Wait, wait, wait," I babble, wincing as pinpricks of pain race across my scalp and my arm burns. "You promised Ichabod you'd take me back with you, right? And you don't break promises, Lakyn. You always keep your promises."

"And I'm about to keep one right now," he answers with a low, rolling chuckle, as I feel him undoing his belt.

Fuck, fuck, fuck.

He shoves my face back into the bed, his knees pinning my legs with more than enough force to leave bruises. The lingering scent of Aftyn in the sheets is getting steadily overwhelmed by the copper odor of blood. It's coming from my arm, soaked into his clothes, coating his hands, his arms, and the hatchet next to us that I know I can't risk yet. I'd never be able to hit him at this angle. I just have to wait, and it's not the first time I've taken it up the ass.

I can handle this.

I can handle Lakyn goddamn Meyer. I won't be one of his mewling whores begging for him to stop, and as soon as I get back to Ichabod I'll take him away and we'll leave Lakyn alone and pathetic like he was when I met him.

"This really would be better with some Blondie, but I've waited long enough to hear you enjoy my dick, Trixie." The sound of him spitting makes my muscles tense, but I force a deep breath.

"No one enjoys your goddamn dick, Lakyn!" I scream, but the solid hit to the back of my head makes me bite my tongue and I taste blood as he laughs and prods my ass with his cock, which is definitely larger than I remember.

"Everyone loves my dick. Hell, Ichabod has been taking it like a champ since you sold him to me, and you'll realize how much you like it in a minute."

I try to say 'no,' but it comes out as a garbled mess that ends in a guttural shout as Lakyn forces his way into my ass with one brutal thrust, pain shooting through me as my back muscles lock up in protest.

"Fuuucckkkk… yeah. You're so goddamn tight." He pulls back and thrusts even harder, ripping me open, but with my mangled tongue I can't do more than groan as he brutalizes me. "Bleeding already, Trix? Guess these sun bitches didn't like to try out your ass, huh?"

Go to hell.

I don't deserve this. I'm above this, and as soon as Lakyn finishes I'm going to slit his fucking throat and bathe in his blood. Then I can rebuild this place and bury this darkness six feet under along with Lakyn Meyer.

FOURTEEN

Gods In the Desert pt. 2

LAKYN

The way this bitch is struggling, howling, and bucking makes me fuck her even harder. Once upon a time, Beatrix St. Germain was the one thing I always wanted, and now that I have her, it seems like a waste of a good fuck.

That doesn't mean I'm going to let her off easy.

"L… a… k—"

"Shut up," I bark at her as I raise her hips, grab a fistful of her hair, and keep thrusting my dick into her hole. She should be fucking honored that I'm the kind of man that keeps my word, otherwise she never would have had the chance to experience me like this.

Trixie tries to clench as best as she can to try and do me some damage, but I let go of her hip and punch her in the back of her head to get her to relax. She lets out a pained moan as I burrow even deeper, the blood coating my dick adding a nice touch to my finally getting the one thing I know I earned so many years ago.

A bead of sweat rolls down the side of my face as I thrust harder and faster. I can feel myself getting close, and since this is always about me and never *them*, I couldn't care less if she gets hers.

"You about ready to feel the glory of the Light fill you, bitch?" I snarl as I dig my fingers into her flesh.

She's crying at this point, but it's mixed with strange mewls of pleasure. Half-light, half-Satanic wannabe, all wrapped up in a tiny little package.

What more could a guy ask for?

A few more thrusts of well-placed rage and I let out a low growl as I fill her ass with my cum.

My breath comes in short pants and a chuckle escapes me. She probably thinks I'm done now, but I've waited far too long for this moment to just let it pass so damn quickly.

I shove Trixie away from me and look down at my dick. A smile begins to creep across my lips as I figure she could do with one last humiliation before she goes to the Light or whatever.

Reaching down, I roughly turn her onto her back and laugh when I see her tear-stained face, red with pain, and somehow still stark with the hope that she'll live to see Ichabod again.

But she doesn't deserve that.

Not after becoming a Sun Fucker and breaking his heart by not remembering him. The one fucking life that she destroyed still hinging on the hope of her fixing it—*that* is a privilege she doesn't deserve.

"Now, suck my dick nice and clean. You know I can't go back to Ichabod with any evidence on me, and if you're thinking of biting me, just know that I'm thinking of snapping your neck," I tell her with a grin.

When she doesn't make a move toward true glory, I shrug and move to straddle her, then shove my cock down her throat.

Trixie gags instantly, her eyes widen, and she begins to sputter for air, her hands wildly swatting at my legs.

"You're such a pussy," I say in a thick voice. "You really don't deserve to experience me anymore than you already have."

She closes her eyes tightly as a sob escapes her, and I lean down to place a hand on her forehead. I keep thrusting my cock in and out of her mouth, laughing each time I hit the back of her throat and making her gag.

Sure, I've had better, but either way, the evidence is being disposed of and that's all I could really ask for.

Suddenly, I feel Trixie's teeth attempting to bear down on me, causing me to pull out immediately. I shake my head and laugh, slapping her forehead with the palm of my hand to get her to look at me.

"You know that wasn't a good idea, right?" I tease with a smirk.

"I want to see Ichabod," she sobs, covering her face with her hands.

"And you will. Kind of."

Trixie lets out another loud sob as I move away from her and get dressed. Ichabod can finish the blowjob she started when we get back home because he'll be so damn grateful that I brought his little pal back that he won't say no.

If anything, he'll probably beg me to let him do it and who would I be to deny him the pleasure?

I run a hand back through my hair once I'm dressed and snap my fingers at the sobbing, bloody, cum-filled bitch on the bed.

"Alright, enough of that; it's annoying. Get up and come get your treat," I tell her.

The last time I said that to her, I smacked her up on Sugar Drops. It made me wonder for a short time if that made me a dealer, but honestly, I just wanted her to shut the fuck up and stop nagging so I could get to know my pot of gold at the end of the bloodstained rainbow.

If I didn't like his personality, I would have fucked and killed him, but he grew on me. Kind of like cancer, and even though I knew I could have gotten rid of him, I've been riding it out ever since.

Literally and figuratively speaking.

I begin to inspect my fingernails, Trixie a blur in the background but still on my radar, and then sigh when she decides that cry babying her way through this might stave off the inevitable.

Baby, that reminds me.

"On your feet, Your Holiness," I snarl at her as I reach for her leg and yank. She drops onto the floor with a dull thud and covers her face as she cowers on her ass.

This is boring.

I've never seen her act like this even when she got the boy smacked up and raped by her buddy Sergio.

It's pathetic really and I haven't got the time for this anymore.

I reach down and pull her to her feet by her hair. I always hated this blonde fucking mop, but I'm going to make sure that it's still nice and pretty, sans golden pointy things—because Ichabod always loved looking at this sow.

"Hey, I'll tell you what," I say as I reach into my pocket and light up another smoke. When Trixie drops her hands and looks at me like the blubbering mess she is, I smile. "If you promise that you'll be good for Ichabod, I'll take you back and we can forget any of this ever happened."

"I promise," she sobs almost immediately, and I laugh.

"Good girl, Now…" I say as I crack my neck and reach for my favorite hatchet. "Arms out to the side. I gotta take you back the way he remembers you, you know."

Trixie does as she's told without so much as giving it a second thought, and when she drops her chin to her chest, I shake my head.

"Uh, uh, bitch. You're not gonna wanna miss this," I tell her in a low, even tone.

The second she looks up at me again, I flick my smoke at her bed, grip the hatchet in both hands, and slam it into her belly. Ichabod would never have recognized her if that shit inside of her started to grow after a while, so I'm taking care of it before he even gets the chance to be disappointed over it.

Her eyes bulge as she reaches for her new, little wound and I crouch down to size her up. The problem is that while I'm sure I got rid of the disappointment, I'm not entirely sure that seeing the gash actually have one is going to do him any good either.

"Hey, Trixie?" I ask as I stand back up and roll my shoulders. She staggers on her feet, struggling to look into my eyes, and I smile.

"This is from Ichabod, but it's more for me."

With a loud grunt, I raise the hatchet and bury it into her throat.

IT TOOK some time to lop her head off her tight little body, but I did a fairly decent job. Her hair is all in place, and I left the crown behind because it's not like Ichabod would recognize that anyway.

The only thing missing before I get going again is Red.

As I walk out of the Fuck House of Light, Trixie's head gripped firmly in one of my hands, I begin to hum. I have no idea where the cactus thing is, but I don't think I'm gonna have to look very far.

Clearing my throat, I lay my hatchet on the ground and put two fingers into my mouth, letting out a shrill whistle.

"Lakyn!"

I roll my eyes and sigh when I hear Red's voice in the distance coming toward me.

She's like a loyal puppy that loves her master no matter how many times she gets kicked.

90970000090000000900000000009090000007000000000000000000000000009000

I retrieve my weapon and glance around until I see that hair of hers skipping toward me, then I grin.

"Kinda makes you wish the sun fuckers were still alive to see this, eh?" I call out to her, raising Trixie's head.

Red stops skipping, her eyes widening in disbelief for a second before she breaks out into a run and wraps her arms around me when she reaches me.

I grunt from the pressure she's applying and let out a sigh. My hands are full so I can't shove her off, and when she makes her little declaration, I feel like maybe I haven't killed enough people today.

"Oh, Lakyn. Now we can be together forever!"

I glance down at her, roll my eyes again, then shrug repeatedly until she lets go.

And if that isn't enough to keep my dick from getting hard ever again, suddenly I hear what sounds like a number of air horns going off at once.

I glare at Red to keep her in place, then look over to the left. It seems that I didn't kill enough of the Sun Fuckers to scare the rest off like I thought, but I think I've done a good enough job of putting a little dent in their operations.

Without The Daughter of Bullshit, they'll all probably go back home and try to get off the smack water.

I can't help but think that I'm a great guy since I keep helping people get clean.

"Do me a favor," I say to Red, glancing at her quickly. "Go inside and rip a piece of Trixie's dress off. And if you can find a box, even better."

I eye the gathering crowd with amusement and shake my head.

And Trixie's too for good measure.

They look like the world just collapsed around them and I guess I'm supposed to give a shit, but I don't.

After about ten minutes of keeping them crying and blubbering by swinging Trixie's head at them a few times, Red finally shows back up.

She's got a box and some ribbon.

This is gonna be the best present he ever received, I think with a grin as I set Trixie's head inside of it and make quick work of wrapping it up.

FIFTEEN

No One Else But Us

DAPHNE

I giggled when Lakyn backed his car into a row of the sun people. Served them right for trying to chase after us.

I think it has to do with Trixie being in the car, but that serves her right too. She tried to be better than Lakyn, tried to prove that she always would be, but he showed her.

I feel much better after drinking some of the cactus water, and as I glance over at Lakyn and rest a hand on his arm, I know he sees it too.

I wish that the gentle evil would still swim circles of gold around him. I wish it would expel with each exhalation of his cigarette, but I'm happy with what we have, and I know that no one will be able to take it from us.

"Isn't this great?" I ask him after he swats my hand away. He'll learn to love me in time, so I don't mind him pushing me away for now. We're meant for each other and he knows it as much as I do.

"What's that?" he inquires in that bored tone of his that I've come to adore.

"We finally did it," I reply gleefully.

Lakyn glances at me and arches an eyebrow. "We?"

"Yeah," I say tucking my hair behind my ears and turning to face him. I tuck my legs underneath myself and smile widely. "Aftyn is dead, Willa is dead, and Trixie is too! Now it'll be just us forever!"

He smirks as he flicks the ashes off the end of his cigarette, then clears his throat as he turns his attention back toward the road.

"And what makes you think that Red?" he asks, barely containing a laugh.

I blink in confusion a few times.

I've done the math for him—I'm not sure what else he expects me to say.

"Everyone that could ever come between us is gone now," I respond in confusion.

"Almost."

He gives me a knowing, sly grin and I smile again. I had almost forgotten about Ichabod, but that seems to be the flavor of the past few days, anyway.

Two scoops of who the hell is Ichabod, please.

But then I get a great idea.

"I can do it if you can't," I tell Lakyn coyly as I begin to twirl my hair around my finger.

"Do what?"

"Take care of Ichabod, obviously."

He looks like he's mulling the offer over. He knows what I can do—all he has to do is give me the go ahead and I'll get the job done. I wouldn't expect him to be able to handle it himself because they've had so much history, but I barely know the man and I'm more than capable.

Lakyn sucks his teeth as he glances into the rearview mirror, then eases his car to the side of the road.

He motions with his head for me to exit the car and I do, eagerly meeting him in the front. He looks me up and down for a moment, rubbing his chin thoughtfully before he shrugs.

"What makes you think I can't do that myself?" he asks evenly.

"Because… you would have done it already."

"And I haven't," he confirms as he crosses his arms over his chest.

I take a step back in confusion, but quickly regain the ground I lost and wrap my arms around his waist, look up into his beautiful blue eyes, and smile happily.

"Okay, he can stay with us as long as he doesn't get in the way," I agree.

Lakyn drapes his arms around my shoulders, lowers his face toward mine, and I close my eyes in anticipation of feeling his lips. I'm almost shaking with the excitement of knowing that he agrees with me.

"Not in this lifetime, baby," he whispers hotly against my lips. Giving me a rough shove, he spins me around, rips my pants down and bends me over the hood of his car. "But I will thank you for giving me the heads up about the kid and the bitch."

"What—Ouch!"

Lakyn laughs as he thrusts his dick deep into my ass and begins thrusting. I try to claw at his wrists—he's giving me the one thing I've been dying for since I met him, but it hurts so much because he's not giving me a chance to—

"How's that dick feel, Red?" he grunts as he pushes deeper into me. "Everything you thought it would be?"

I can't help but start crying.

If not from the pain alone, but from the feeling of being used all over again. I thought Lakyn loved me, cared about me, and he's treating me like any other bastard that's ever looked at me and thought I was weak.

"Stop!" I manage to screech through a sob which only makes him laugh harder and thrust faster.

"You sure about that?" he growls as he reaches forward and grabs me by the hair, pulling me back against him.

"Please!" I scream.

"What a waste," he whispers into my ear.

When he pulls his dick out of my ass, I can feel the blood slowly running down my leg, but I'm much too ashamed and scared to move.

I can hear Lakyn pull his zipper back up, the sound of his shoes crunching against the gravel, followed by the sound of a door opening and closing.

A few seconds later, I hear him approaching me again and I close my eyes tightly. I don't want to believe it, but I know what's coming next. I should have taken a knife with me... but I trusted him. I wanted to be free so badly, with Lakyn Meyer, but that's not going to happen. It's not my destiny.

"End of the road, Red. It was fun while it lasted, but just so you know, I've had better."

The words hurt, but not as much as the hatchet, and I don't even fight it. A life without him wouldn't be a life at all.

Choking on my own blood, I can't talk, and I can't see anything except the dirt, but just before the dark swallows me whole I remember the two words that first bound me to him.

Hail Lakyn.

SIXTEEN

Old Friends

LAKYN

I run a hand back through my hair as I sing along to the song on the radio. I reach over and rest a hand on the box that's holding Ichabod's present and drum my fingers to the beat.

"I always told you this would happen, Trixie. Guess you thought I was lying to you, but you should have known better," I admonish her cheerfully.

The last two weeks have been longer than they should have been and maybe even a little harder, but it's nice to know that when push comes to shove, I can still boogie with the best of them.

Hell, even better than most.

I left Red on the side of the road somewhere near the hippie camp. I figure they can take the rap for that one. Especially since they're all smacked up, they'll more than likely think it was a sign from Trixie's dearly departed body.

With a grin, I reach for a smoke and light up, then take a well-deserved, long drag.

It'll be nice to be able to go home and relax now. It took me twenty years to get to this point, and now there's really nothing left to wonder about.

Trixie's ass was nice and tight, but that was more than likely due to the kid not knowing that women have more than one hole.

He's dead; not that he ever should have been alive, or even knew how to fucking live. I can't say that I was impressed with him, and I wasn't planning on giving him a chance regardless.

One Meyer is more than enough for this world to behold, and as usual, I came out on top.

Top; that reminds me.

"Hey, Trixie, think Ichabod will be happy to see you again?" I ask with a laugh. "He thought I lied to him when I came back without you, but I couldn't tell him that you didn't remember him. It would have broken his ex-junkie heart and then I'd have to service myself until he got over it. I think this is a much better way to patch up that little tiff we had, don't you?"

I glance at the box and chuckle.

For the first time in her miserable fucking life, the bitch has nothing to say.

Granted, she still has her nose to look down on people, but only if I point it that way.

Bitch, I think irritably as the grin on my lips falters slightly.

I never did give a shit about Beatrix St. Germain or Ichabod Foster.

This was nothing more than me proving to both of them that out of the three of us, I'm the one that has the balls to do what needs to be done.

He'll probably have a hissy fit when he opens his present, but all he said was that he wanted to see her again.

He never mentioned *how*.

I just hope he's got the house cleaned up by the time I get home otherwise he's gonna have more than just a window to reimburse me for.

Taking a deep breath, I take my hand off the box and place it on the steering wheel.

Twenty years?

I've spent twenty years with someone?

With an eye roll, I wonder if he thinks it means more than it actually does.

Honestly, I just don't feel like breaking any one new in and he knows what I like even when I don't.

Playing houseboy by cleaning up the place, making sure I've always got a hot meal, and some tight holes to fuck is plenty for me.

Of course, if he manages to find anymore 'children' of mine, he's gonna wish he left them wherever the fuck they were.

But I think there's a lesson to be learned in all of this.

It just so happens to be that no matter what happens, no one will ever be able to top what I can do to—or for—someone.

And the sub-lesson is to let sleeping dogs lie. Some monsters are better left resting than being fucked with.

That's when things tend to get messy.

And messy is where I always fucking shine.

With a smirk, I rest my head back against the seat, take another drag of my smoke, and press down on the gas pedal.

God, I'm fucking amazing.

SEVENTEEN

A Promise Kept

ICHABOD

I sit up with a start when I hear a car door open and close outside. I should know better than to run to the window with hope in my heart, but I really don't think that Lakyn would have left and returned again with empty hands.

I don't want to be with Bea anymore—not in the way I did when I was a kid, I just want to sit and talk with her for a few hours. See how she's been, ask her about any adventures she's been on, and then ask Lakyn if she can stay the night.

I used to love curling up with Bea on cold nights out in the street when we were younger. There would be times that Zoe would kick me out of the house for one reason or another, so I'd find an alley to sleep in and somehow, Bea always found me.

I never did follow her home like she wanted me to, though. I never felt like I was clean enough or even good enough to walk through her damn doors, and now I'm wishing harder than I ever have before that she'll walk through mine.

I run my hands over my face as I finally force myself off the couch and walk over to the window. Peeking through the curtains, I sigh heavily when I realize it was just one of the neighbors and that Lakyn isn't back yet.

Now I'm wondering if he'll ever come back again. I know that I went too far with what I said to him and smashing his stuff up, and I know he hasn't forgiven me for that yet, but I hope he understands.

I would imagine that if he cared about anyone other than himself, he'd react the same way that I did, though I know that would never happen.

He's far too calm and collected to show when something is bothering him which is why it scared the shit out of me when he retreated to his room and stayed there after he came back the first time.

I half expected him to kill me.

I would have welcomed it because that would have been better than being in a world without Bea. Even if she was closer than I had assumed this whole time, at least she's out there somewhere and that thought alone has always kept me going.

It's just being given the opportunity to see her again, something I never would have thought could happen until Aftyn showed up... taking it away would be crueler than anything Lakyn could ever do to me.

Or has done, and he's been pretty fucked-up about how he's treated me since day one.

But I learned to adapt to it.

I can see his triggers before he feels them coming and I always back off. I've come to accept that I'll never be anything more to him than a whipping boy and I'm fine with it.

I'd like him to maybe tell me if he feels something for me one day—other than the usual verbal abuse that I'm numb to. Even if it's the smallest thing, it would be nice to hear.

It'll never happen, I think with a heavy sigh as I let the curtain go and turn away.

I'm almost back to the couch when a car horn outside blares a couple of times. I turn so quickly that I almost trip over my own feet as I rush back to the window just in time to see Lakyn pulling into the driveway.

Taking a deep breath, I let go of the curtain again and rush for the front door. I'm hope that he has Bea with him, but if he doesn't, I can't honestly say that I'll be surprised.

Disappointed?

Absolutely, but that's something else I'm starting to become numb to.

Life with Lakyn has been full of disappointments. None for him, of course, but enough to break someone that didn't have the chance to become conditioned to it.

I chew my lower lip nervously as I run my hands back through my hair, then use a shaky hand to pull the front door open.

Stepping out onto the front stoop, I shove my hands into my pockets and nod at him as he exits the car with a half-grin on that devilishly handsome face of his.

Lakyn Meyer is and always will be the most beautiful man I've ever seen, and he knows it.

He used it to his advantage when I first met him. Suckered me hook, line, and sinker into thinking that he was as interested in me as I was him, and I fell for it harder than I'll ever admit.

"Hey," I call out in a shaky tone.

Lakyn rest an arm over the door of his car as he looks at me for a moment, then slams it shut.

I should have known, I think dejectedly when I don't see Bea.

"Guess she didn't wanna come, huh?" I ask in a subdued voice.

"What makes you say that?" he asks as he walks around to the other side of his car.

"Lack of presence," I joke lamely.

"Come on, you should know me better than that," he replies with a chuckle as he opens the passenger side of his door, leans in to grab something, then uses his foot to close it.

"As promised," he announces cheerfully as he approaches me and shoves a box into my hands.

"What?" I ask in confusion.

"Well, you *have* been a good boy lately, with the exception of the nasty little surprise you sprang on me, but I have to hand it to you— that was slick," he tells me with a laugh as he walks by me and claps me on the back.

My hands begin to shake harder as his laugh echoes in the house behind me.

My lower lip starts to tremble as I hold the box, refusing to look down at it.

Lakyn said he kept his promise.

Which means Bea is home.

I can feel my breathing becoming labored as I turn my eyes up toward the sky. Nothing Lakyn has ever done has surprised me, and he even lost the ability to hurt me after being with him this long.

This was the only way he knew he'd be able to do it.

And now… now I don't have a friend left in this world.

Just like he always wanted.

"Get your ass in this fucking house and shut the door," he calls out. "I've had a long couple of days, and I need to blow off some steam."

About Yolanda Olson

Yolanda Olson is a USA Today Bestselling and award-winning author. Born and raised in Bridgeport, CT where she currently resides, she usually spends her time watching her favorite channel, Investigation Discovery. Occasionally, she takes a break to write books and test the limits of her mind. Also an avid horror movie fan, she likes to incorporate dark elements into the majority of her books.

You can keep in touch with her on Facebook, Twitter, and Instagram

Sign up for her newsletter here.

Also by Yolanda Olson

The Inferno Series:

Inferno

Cinere

Sparks

Embers

The Complete Inferno Series Boxed Set

The Malediction Saga:

Scavengers

Vultures

Carrion

Malediction Codex

Dark M/M:

Death Blooms

A Brush with the Devil

Barren (Carnaval des Ténèbres Book 1)

Deprivation

Where Sleeping Gods Lie

Dark Horror:

BONES

Nefarious

Hunger

Moments in Oblivion

Erotic Horror:

Strangers

Ghost Flowers

The Beast of Bondi Beach Duet

Creep

Deep Blue

8 Days for Salvation

Wrong Side of Heaven

anatomy

Milk and Honey

Delicate Things

One Hundred Saints

agony

Hollow

Gothic Romance:

The Lies Between Us

A Serenade of Fireflies

Martyris

Co-Writes:

Otter's Toy Box

Abattoir

Invictus

Scorched

Dark Holiday Themed:

Bastards and Baubles: A Very Villainous
Christmas

Press Play

About Jennifer Bene

Jennifer Bene is a *USA Today* bestselling author of dangerously sexy and deviously dark romance. From BDSM, to Suspense, Dark Romance, and Thrillers—she writes it all. Always delivering a twisty, spine-tingling journey with the promise of a happily-ever-after.

Don't miss a release! Sign up for the newsletter to get new book alerts (and a free welcome book) at: http://jenniferbene.com/newsletter

---

You can find her online throughout social media with username @jbeneauthor and on her website: www.jenniferbene.com

Also by Jennifer Bene

The Thalia Series (Dark Romance)

Security Binds Her *(Thalia Book 1)*

Striking a Balance *(Thalia Book 2)*

Salvaged by Love *(Thalia Book 3)*

Tying the Knot *(Thalia Book 4)*

The Thalia Series: The Complete Collection

The Beth Series (Dark Romance)

Breaking Beth *(Beth Book 1)*

Fragile Ties Series (Dark Romance)

Destruction *(Fragile Ties Book 1)*

Inheritance *(Fragile Ties Book 2)*

Redemption *(Fragile Ties Book 3)*

Dangerous Games Series (Dark Mafia Romance)

Early Sins *(A Dangerous Games Prequel)*

Lethal Sin *(Dangerous Games Book 1)*

Standalone Dark Romance

Imperfect Monster

Corrupt Desires

Deviant Attraction: A Dark and Dirty Collection

Reign of Ruin

Mesmer

Jasmine

Crazy Broken Love

Standalone BDSM Ménage Romance

The Invitation

Reunited

Dark Suspense / Horror

Burned: An Inferno World Novella

Scorched: A New Beginning

Noxious *(Anathema Book 1)*

Mephitic *(Anathema Book 2)*

Viperous *(Anathema Book 3)*

Appearances in the Black Light Series (BDSM Romance)

Black Light: Exposed *(Black Light Series Book 2)*

Black Light: Valentine Roulette *(Black Light Series Book 3)*

Black Light: Roulette Redux *(Black Light Series Book 7)*

Black Light: Celebrity Roulette *(Black Light Series Book 12)*

Black Light: Charmed *(Black Light Series Book 15)*

Black Light: Roulette War *(Black Light Series Book 16)*

Black Light: The Beginning *(Black Light Series Book 17.5)*

Black Light: Unbound *(Black Light Series Book 18)*

Books Released As Cassandra Faye

Daughters of Eltera Series (Dark Fantasy Romance)

Fae *(Daughters of Eltera Book 1)*

Tara *(Daughters of Eltera Book 2)*

Standalone Paranormal Romance

Hunted *(The Dirty Heroes Collection Book 13)*

One Crazy Bite

Dangerous Magic